THE SMALL PARTY

Lillian Beckwith

ARROW BOOKS

Arrow Books Limited
20 Vauxhall Bridge Road, London SW1V 2SA

An imprint of Random Century Group

London Melbourne Sydney Auckland
Johannesburg and agencies throughout
the world

First published in Great Britain by Century 1989
Arrow edition 1990

Printed and bound in Great Britain by
Courier International Ltd, Tiptree, Essex

ISBN 0 09 968620 1

1

Closing the door of the house gently so as not to wake the children Ruth followed her sister-in-law out to the parked brake. At the garden gate the two women paused, their gaze venerating the lingering radiance of a sunset which still enriched the waters of the bay. After a moment of awed silence Ruth observed, 'Aren't we fortunate, Jeannie? I mean being able to see the glorious sunsets we get here; the sky almost pulsing with colour and yet the sea so hushed and tranquil. You know there are times when the sheer splendour of a sunset like there's been this evening seems to wrench at my senses and sort of coerce them into an even deeper appreciation of my luck in living here, despite the disadvantages.'

'You mean despite the disadvantages of being so vulnerable to isolation and virtually crippled by strikes on the mainland over which our government has no jurisdiction whatsoever?' Jeannie retorted bitterly. 'The shipping strike was bad enough but a general strike that affects all transport is just too much to endure. Oh,' she tutted; 'I'm sorry I'm letting myself get worked up,' she apologized. 'Yes, of course I do agree it's a lovely island and the sunsets, when we can see them, can be truly spectacular. And no, I wouldn't want to live anywhere else,' she conceded. 'But for people like me who are dependent on livestock for our income, shortage of feeding stuffs soon leads to shortage of the ready.' She sighed. 'If only more of the island's mills were still operating we could be reasonably self-sufficient but it's too late to moan about that.'

Ruth regarded her sister-in-law gravely. 'You're not

short of the ready, are you, Jeannie?' she asked. 'You know Dave and I would. . . .'

'Nothing like that yet anyway but I do resent not having enough food to do the poultry really well. They're not just my living, they're my pride.'

'I've not heard you complain before, Jeannie,' Ruth said. 'Are you truly beginning to run short of supplies? You did say when the strike started you were well stocked up.'

'I was then but I didn't think it was going to develop into a general strike on the mainland or that it would last so long. No one did, did they? We've suffered from strikes of one sort or another before but never to the extent when vital supplies ran out. Things weren't so bad while our own fishing boats were able to bring in a trickle of supplies, but now they're facing so much aggro from the strikers picketing the ports they're refusing to go across.'

'Oh, Jeannie, I've been so selfish,' Ruth exclaimed penitently. 'You've been keeping us so well supplied with butter and eggs and cheese and vegetables we've hardly noticed the shortages, so surely there must be something we can do for you in return?'

'Nothing really, I think,' answered Jeannie. 'You already give me whatever household scraps you have.'

'I could persuade the neighbours to save their scraps for you and I could collect them whenever I could get some petrol,' Ruth volunteered.

'That would help a little, I dare say,' Jeannie acknowledged. She frowned. 'I opened the last of the sacks of grain yesterday and there's no more where that came from. Not until the next harvest, or until this strike's over and we can import supplies again. With this present spell of good weather the cows are getting plenty of grass so there's more than enough milk for the calves. They can do without extras like calf nuts but I've already had to cut down on the poultry food. If I have to cut down any more they'll respond by laying fewer eggs and that means less for market.' Her expression became set. 'There's a rumour now that the government may have to reduce even the priority petrol ration and if that happens I'll maybe not have enough to run the brake which will make it impossible to get my eggs to the retailers. At least I suppose that will solve one problem,' she ended with cynical abruptness.

'And pose another,' Ruth pointed out.

'It would mean plenty of chicken dinners.' Jeannie's tone was trenchant.

'I do wish I could do more to help,' Ruth said worriedly, but a moment later her expression brightened. 'I know!' she burst out. 'The last message I had from Dave was that *Moonwind*'s refit was nearing completion. He could be home within a few days. Now if I can get a message to him in time I'll ask him to load *Moonwind* with as many sacks of grain as he can get and bring it down for you.'

'Even if you can get a message to him is it likely there's grain available?' Jeannie asked doubtfully.

'Dave said there doesn't seem to be much in the way of shortages locally. Not up there where he is. I'm sure he'd find a way of getting hold of some supplies.'

'Is there a chance of getting in touch with him?' Jeannie still sounded dubious.

'I can usually manage to get our coastguard to get a signal through to him fairly quickly,' Ruth said. 'I don't think he's at home at the moment but I can pop a note through his letter box this evening so he'll see it as soon as he gets back. If I mark it "Urgent" he'll attend to it as soon as he can.'

'Gosh! That would be simply splendid,' Jeannie enthused. 'I shall sleep easier tonight just for knowing there's a possibility.' Getting into the brake she settled herself in the driving seat. 'Aren't you well placed, living just across the road from the coastguard?' she remarked.

'In more ways than one,' Ruth agreed warmly. 'He's such a nice man and the children are very fond of him. He's Uncle Guardie to them.'

Jeannie closed the door of the brake and switched on the engine.

'Well, once again thank you for coming to help celebrate Susan's birthday,' Ruth said. 'It's been wonderful having you with us.'

'I've enjoyed it enormously,' Jeannie assured her. 'I've had a super day and I would have hated to miss a moment of it.'

'The children do so love having you come to see us and Susan's birthday picnic wouldn't have gone with nearly such a swing if you hadn't been with us. You're such a good organizer.'

'Call me "bossy" and you'll be nearer the truth,' refuted Jeannie lightly.

'Whatever you like to call it, it's something the children respond to eagerly,' Ruth insisted. 'I only wish I'd been blessed with a stronger streak of it.'

Jeannie glanced at Ruth affectionately. 'Oh, you've got what it takes,' she comforted. 'It's just that you're still feeling run down after your illness. You'll be fit again soon enough and bouncing with verve and energy.'

'I certainly hope so,' Ruth said.

'Of course you will,' Jeannie maintained firmly. 'See you next week then, petrol and poultry permitting. But seriously, Ruth, if you do feel the least bit ropey don't hesitate to give me a ring. I can always come and give you a hand.'

'Not on your meagre petrol ration,' Ruth reminded her.

'I've still got my old bike, thank goodness!' Jeannie retorted.

'It's good of you but you've more than enough to do at your own place without having my frailties on your mind,' Ruth countered. 'I shall be perfectly all right. Simon and Heather have been especially helpful since Dave left and Susan's been trying hard to be very grown-up.'

'Maybe so, but I promised my big brother I'd do my best to keep an eye on you while he was away, so please say you'll give me a ring if I can help.' They smiled at each other understandingly. 'I'll do that certainly,' granted Ruth.

Jeannie let in the clutch but Ruth raised a restraining hand. 'Jeannie, I must say again how good it was of you to give Susan Gruntly Finny for her birthday. As you know she's been captivated by him ever since she first discovered him sitting on the window seat in your bedroom but now she's got him for her very own it's easy to see she's ecstatic.'

Jeannie turned in her seat and switched off the engine. 'You truly think so?' she questioned with evident relief. 'You're sure she wasn't a bit disappointed that she wasn't given a brand new teddy bear?' she pressed, and, reassured by Ruth's emphatic head-shake, she went on, 'I did try to get her a new one but the strike has hit the toy shops particularly hard. They're almost denuded of stock and all I was offered was a teddy that was pink and perfumed.'

The two women grimaced at each other.

'I can assure you Susan is absolutely delighted,' Ruth asserted.

'Well, yes, she did seem pleased, didn't she?' admitted Jeannie with a faint blush of embarrassment. 'I have to admit I was more than a little doubtful about including Gruntly among her presents, but since choice was so limited I thought I'd try tarting him up with a bit more stuffing and a pair of jeans and a cap to cover the worst of the wear and then I'd see what she thought

9

of him. I was worried she might reject him as a birthday present no matter how much she'd thought of him previously and honestly, Ruth, I was so touched when I saw how eager she was to claim him.'

'And she's hardly let go of him since,' Ruth was quick to point out. 'No, Jeannie, don't think for a minute you could have given Susan a more wanted present. You noticed she didn't pay much attention to the other presents you gave her today,' she added a little contritely. 'She will come to be interested in them soon enough, I'm sure, but just at the moment she's totally besotted with Gruntly Finny. I think I can see why too. There's no doubt he's really a very huggable bear.'

'I'm rather glad now I didn't take the ring out of his ear,' Jeannie said. 'I did debate with myself whether or not I should.'

'Oh, I'm so glad you left it,' Ruth approved. 'It made him instantly recognizable to Susan despite his new rig-out.' She paused. 'Wasn't it Dave who put the ring in Gruntly's ear?' she asked. 'I seem to remember his telling me something about it.'

'You're quite right,' Jeannie confirmed. 'It was the first time we went out in Dad's new boat and of course I wouldn't leave Gruntly Finny behind. Dave said then that if Gruntly was to become a sailor bear he ought to wear an ear-ring because all good sailor bears wore ear-rings to bring them luck. Of course anything my big brother told me I never questioned, so we raided Mum's knick-knack box and found this old curtain ring which Dave fixed so firmly to Gruntly's ear that there it's stayed. Not that I minded; I thought it made him look even more handsome.' Jeannie chuckled reminiscently. 'What memories that brings,' she added in an undertone. 'It will no doubt sound pretty daft to you but I don't think I ever outgrew my childhood affection for Gruntly Finny.' Her mouth curved into a wistful smile. 'I suppose the fact that he's still extant makes that obvious. Oh, of course there were times when I was past childhood and in my teens that I forgot all about him but I was always pleased to re-discover him. Mum coaxed but I wouldn't be per-suaded to part with him. I remember once, I must have been nearly eighteen, discovering Gruntly at the bottom of my wardrobe amidst a pile of cast-off clothing destined for the local jumble sale. He looked so forlorn I was stricken with remorse and I actually cried, even at that age. I tied him to a cushion and sat him on a chair in my bedroom so he'd never be lost again, and there he stayed until I married Jim and we moved into the cottage.' She permitted herself a wan smile. 'Jim used to tease me a little at first about hanging on to Gruntly but we both knew that we were hoping it wouldn't be too long before he'd be claimed by a new owner.' Her voice trembled.

'It doesn't sound at all daft to me,' Ruth assured her. 'It sounds perfectly natural. My own teddy bear was cuddled to disintegration, more or less,' she confessed ruefully. 'Kids do seem to let teddy bears burrow into their affections, don't they? More so than any other toys, I mean.'

'Mmm,' Jeannie agreed. 'But I can't help being intrigued by Susan's delight at being given my old teddy bear for a birthday present when normally she would have been expecting something brand new.'

'But that's the point,' Ruth reasoned. 'It's because he was your bear when you were a little girl that makes him appeal so strongly to Susan. I think she's come to regard him as a grown-up bear that she can trust and confide in. Gruntly isn't just a strange new bear from a toyshop which anyone could have had. He's Gruntly Finny and very special. Almost a collateral if you see what I'm trying to explain. I'm certain she's going to cling to him as devotedly as you did,' she added.

11

'Bless her!' said Jeannie tenderly. 'She really is a little darling.' After a moment's reflection she added, 'I adore all three of them naturally but Susan seems to have an extra little touch of winsomeness that tends to reach out and coil itself around one's affections. I suppose it's because she's the youngest.' For a moment her fingers gripped the steering wheel. 'I'd have wanted one of mine to be like her.' Her voice trailed to a low murmur.

'Tell me,' Ruth hastened to interpose, 'how come he's Gruntly Finny? It sounds so upper crust, one would expect it to be hyphenated,' she observed lightly.

'Oh, that's easily accounted for,' Jeannie elucidated with a grin. 'Gruntly was given to me by my Uncle Finlay, so to begin with I called him Finny, the nearest I could get to saying Finlay then. When I found he gave a fascinating growl every time I pressed his tummy he became Growly Finny. Eventually, after what I suppose was a surfeit of tummy squeezing his growl petered into a short grunt and then it was Dave who began calling him Gruntly Finny and thereafter the name stuck.'

'So that's it,' Ruth accepted. 'But I shall have to try and coax Susan not to make him grunt too much when Tansy's around, shan't I, old girl?' she said, looking fondly at the shaggy terrier standing beside her. 'Poor Tansy seemed to think she was being threatened. I was quite startled at the way she reacted to it, because as you know yourself she's normally such a docile lady, aren't you, old girl?' Tansy acknowledged the question with a wag of her tail.

'I expect she'll quickly get used to being grunted at,' said Jeannie, re-starting the engine. 'But I really must get back now or the polecats will be slaughtering my chickens. Cheerio then, and I shall hope to see you next week.'

'Petrol permitting,' Ruth reminded her.

'I shall be okay. I was lucky today. I managed to get my full quota at the garage this morning so, barring crises, I should be able to cope until my next allocation is due.'

'I miss not being able to use the car more than everything else,' Ruth grumbled. 'But Dave may be back by the end of next week and I'm hoping he'll bring some fuel. I'm keeping my fingers crossed for that to happen,' she shouted above the noise of the engine.

'I'll join you in that,' declared Jeannie, holding up her crossed fingers. 'Bye then.'

Ruth watched the brake until it had turned out on to the main road. She heard its surge of speed steady and then recede into the distance. Dear, brave Jeannie, she mused as she went back into the house. Jeannie who was invariably kind and caring; so ready to offer help when help was needed; so competent, so popular and yet so tragically lonely.

Three years previously Jeannie had been a euphorically happy young wife, sharing enthusiastically her husband Jim's ambition to transform the small neglected hill farm they had bought into the totally organic holding they were convinced would prove to be their most rewarding approach to the farming life. The idea of keeping battery hens had offended them as indeed had the intensive rearing of any animals. On their farm no sucking calf would be torn from its distraught mother; there would be no chemical fertilizers used on the land. Their vision had been idealistic, but they were young and strong and their shared idealism had given them the courage to pursue their goal regardless of the friendly inducements and the often satirical advice offered by their more practical neighbours. Together they had worked hard and cheerfully, exulting in each small success until the day, only twelve months after they had embarked on their planned venture, Jim had been killed in a freak accident. In seconds Jeannie's happy world had been shattered. Devastated by grief she had lost the child she had begun to suspect was forming in her womb, but like an automaton she had carried on with the daily work of the farm, her stricken eyes and dull responses evincing the only clues to her suffering. To her anxious family it had seemed too long a time before they could discern any sign of her recovering from the tragedy, but eventually they had come to perceive traces of a return of resoluteness in her manner, and had been able to comfort themselves that in battling through her ordeal she had been stirred to undertake alone the task of fulfilling the dream she and her beloved husband had once shared.

Back in the house Ruth closed the door carefully. She ached for sleep but first she had to write a brief note for the coastguard and pop it into his letter box. That done, she waited only to lock up, settle Tansy into her basket and check that the kettle was full ready for morning, before she mounted the stairs to her own bedroom, pausing only to take a swift precautionary peep into each child's room as she passed.

In the gentle warmth of the June night the children were sleeping peacefully, cheeks flushed, tendrils of hair clinging to moist brows, young bodies spent after the absorbing activities of the day. On their beds the thin coverlets lay pushed to their feet half concealing cherished toys unwittingly released from sleep-slackened fingers.

Simon, eight years old and the eldest of her children, occupied one of the two double rooms. It was typically a boy's room, the mint-green walls serving as a random gallery for the pinned and pasted pictures of boats and cars and planes, while the floor space between the foot of his bed and the window was ringed by a car-racing track.

Heather, aged six, had the single room across the landing, and here the pale blue walls were profusely decorated with pictures of beguiling kittens and puppies, of horses and birds and wildlife. The deeper blue ceiling was studded with foil stars so she could pretend, as she drifted into sleep, that she was seeing the night sky beyond the open flap of a tent, the desire to become a Brownie having lodged in her mind since the day she had been taken by Brown Owl to watch the exploits of the local pack.

Susan, whose fourth birthday they had been celebrating that day, was in the small room which adjoined that of her parents and here a colourful frieze of nursery rhyme characters was the borderline between the spruce cream paint above and the pale blue paint below, now besmirched with a miscellany of chalk daubs and scribbles. On the pillow beside Susan's head Gruntly Finny lay with her little finger still hooked in his ear-ring. A gentle smile hovered around Ruth's lips. She had so much to be grateful for. In her own room she drew the curtains across the window, slipped into her nightdress and, after giving her hair only two of the customary fifty strokes of the brush, she slid under the bedcover and began to murmur her ritual thanks to her Maker, but sleep overwhelmed her before she had come to the end of her first prayer.

2

When the first muffled noises rumbled over the moonlit Port, Ruth stirred grudgingly. Her mind, thick with sleep, registered the sound only as distant thunder and, willing it to skirt the island as thunderstorms so often did, she allowed herself to relax into light slumber, confident she would waken at the first whimper of distress from the children.

At the third and distinctly louder rumble, Heather, always the lightest sleeper of the children, shot into wakefulness. First groping for the comfort of her toy penguin, she then pulled the cord of the light switch that hung above her bed. Tumbling out of bed she ran swiftly across the landing to Simon's room. 'Simon!' Her whisper was harsh and urgent, and when he did not wake instantly she tapped him smartly on the head with her penguin. 'Simon, please wake up quickly. I can hear thunder and I think I saw lightning. I'm frightened and I want to know if you think it's near enough to wake Mummy.'

At any other time Heather would have rushed straight to her mother with her fear, but it was not long since Mummy had been poorly and Daddy, who was a fisherman, had talked seriously to the children before he'd had to take his fishing boat *Moonwind* up to Grandpa's boatyard in the north of Scotland for her annual refit. He'd stressed that though Mummy was no longer poorly she still needed rest, and he urged them to try not to waken her at night unless they were sure they had a very special reason for doing so. The children had been anxious to heed his appeal to them and now Heather, unsure whether an approaching

16

thunderstorm could be considered a good enough excuse for waking Mummy, wanted her brother's support.

Simon struggled from sleep. 'No!' he decided, after Heather had repeated her question. 'At any rate not until I hear if it's a bad one.'

Like a growl of defiance the rumbling became ominously closer. Heather's taut little body began to shiver uncontrollably. 'Can I get into your bed with you, then? Just for a little minute?' she pleaded and, without waiting for Simon's reply, scrambled in beside him.

'Oh, all right.' Simon tried to sound testy. Because Daddy had explained to him all about thunderstorms and how and why they happened, Simon had convinced himself that there was no need to be afraid of them, but it was a conviction that did not necessarily work without the presence of an adult to witness his lack of fear.

Through the thin summery curtains light filtered vaguely. 'Is it moonlight or is it going to be morning soon?' Heather asked. 'Shall I switch on your light?' She had already pulled the switch before she had finished her question. 'There's a smell like dirty smoke,' she went on to complain. 'It's coming in through your window and it's making me want to cough.'

Simon sat up and sniffed several times. 'Yes, I can smell it too,' he agreed. 'Yuk!' He too grimaced. 'It's strong! Someone must have set a chimney on fire and the smoke's coming this way.'

'Close your window!' Heather ordered in a tone that was made peremptory by fear.

'You can close it if you want to,' countered Simon, sliding down on to the pillow.

'It's your window so you should close it,' argued Heather. 'Anyway,' she confessed. 'I'm too scared.'

'Oh, all right.' Simon was still determined to sound unconcerned. As he sped across the floor he tripped over his racing track and pulled up short against the window sill. Pulling the curtains aside to get at the latch he gave a gasp of astonishment. 'Hi, Heather! Come and look!' he exclaimed excitedly. 'There's a huge ginormous fire down near the harbour. Gosh!' His excitement changed to awe.

Heather needed no second bidding. Quickly she joined him and together they watched with fascinated horror the flares of flame and torrents of sparks twisting and soaring into the darkness above the smoke-shrouded buildings. 'I think we ought to wake Mummy now,' Heather was beginning to say, when there came a brilliant flash followed by an ear-shattering explosion that seemed to them to bounce against the house and leave it shuddering from the impact. Simultaneously the bedside lamp went out. With reckless leaps the children were back on Simon's bed, clinging together in panic and screaming for their Mummy.

'It's all right, my darlings.' Ruth was already hurrying into the room and beaming her pocket torch towards the bed.

'Mummy! It's thundering and lightning and the house shook,' the mingled voices of the two children gabbled excitedly. As they were speaking a shrill wail of sleepy terror came from Susan's room.

'Coming, darling!' Ruth called over her shoulder. To Simon and Heather she said with hasty calm, 'Yes, I heard it but it's only thunder and it'll pass over in a while. You two put on your dressing gowns while I get Susan, then we'll all go downstairs and stay in the kitchen until it's all over.' She sped quickly into Susan's room but Heather was hard on her heels, pulling at her dressing gown and impeding her progress.

'Mummy! Mummy! Please don't leave us alone,' she implored. 'I'm awful, awful frightened.'

'Of course I'm not leaving you alone, except to get Susan. She's frightened too, so come on.' She took

Heather's hand. 'You hold the torch, Heather, so we can see what we're doing,' she instructed. Lifting the now loudly wailing Susan, Ruth held her close, murmuring pacifyingly as she carried her across the landing where Simon waited anxiously. 'Now, Heather, where's your dressing gown?'

'It's in my bedroom,' Heather said. 'I didn't have time to put it on when I ran to Simon's room.'

'Come along then.' Ruth ushered Heather in front of her. Simon, already in his dressing gown, followed.

'There's a ginormous fire down by the harbour,' he told Ruth. 'Look!' He pulled back the landing window curtains and the children heard her sharp intake of breath as she saw the fierce glow in the tormented sky. 'Perhaps the lightning has struck the power station and that's what's made all the lights go out,' Simon suggested.

'More likely to have been a pylon, I should think,' Ruth said. 'Pylons do get struck quite often, I believe.' Simon let the curtain drop back. 'Anyway, it's far away enough from here so we have no need to worry. The fire brigade will soon have it under control.' She strove to keep her voice calm but their fear had already infected her.

'I haven't heard the fire buzzer go off yet,' Simon observed. 'You'd think it would have, wouldn't you?'

'Maybe,' she began, but her voice checked abruptly and they all stiffened as, into the teetering silence, the fire siren howled its belated warning. The moment it had subsided there began a hasty and erratic ringing of the church's single bell, which in turn ceased abruptly as if bidden to silence by the recognizably familiar thuds of the lifeboat maroon. An icy hand seemed to clutch at Ruth's stomach. The fire siren she should have expected to hear; the maroon obviously indicated some peril at sea (though not her husband, thank God!); but the ringing of the church bell at

19

such a hour sounded so uncanny she could think of no rational explanation.

The baffled silence was broken by Simon. 'Mummy,' he asked tensely, 'why is the church bell ringing in the middle of the night?'

Ruth tried to answer him but her voice was trapped in her throat.

'Perhaps it's because it's such a bad thunderstorm,' Heather supplied tentatively. 'And perhaps the vicar thinks everyone will be frightened so he's ringing the bell to remind them that God will look after them and keep them safe.'

'Yes, that's very likely the reason,' Ruth managed to say, feeling curiously grateful for the child's naïve interpretation.

For the sake of the children she knew she must strive to achieve some semblance of calm, despite her shuddering nerves and despite her growing certainty that they were being threatened by something far more sinister than a thunderstorm. She tried to grasp the import of the disparate warnings, for warnings she was now convinced they must be. What menaced them? The Bomb? The thought thrust itself to the front of her mind. No! Please God! Not the Bomb! They had been led to believe there would be no precursor should that come, she reminded herself with a grisly sense of relief. Could there have been a big explosion at the gasworks? Or at the generating station? Either could have set off some sort of chain reaction which could account for the fires and explosions. Or could they be the result of some natural phenomenon not hitherto experienced in this part of the world? An earthquake possibly? Didn't earthquakes begin with the noise of rumbling before they climaxed? Fears mounted so easily in the dark that the barest possibilities loomed like probabilities. She tried to combat them by thinking of the calm reasoning voice of her husband. Oh, if only Dave was here, she yearned.

'Are we ready to go down then, now?' Simon wanted to know.

'Just a moment while I think,' she bade him, closing her eyes briefly while she tried to concentrate her thoughts. 'We could do with a better torch than this one,' she decided. 'It might be some time before the electricity's restored and this little one of mine won't last long.'

'I've got the big torch Daddy gave me for Christmas,' Simon cut in eagerly. 'It's in my toy cupboard.'

'Are the batteries good?' Ruth asked.

'They should be.' Simon sounded fairly confident. 'It's not all that long ago I got new batteries for it and I've hardly used it since.'

Ruth hoped he was right. 'Let's go and get it,' she said, shepherding them back into Simon's room.

Heather tried to push in front, exclaiming, 'I can find it quickly. I know where it is.'

'No, Heather.' Her brother elbowed her roughly out of his way. 'It's my torch and it's my toy cupboard and if you know what's in it you must have been sneaking,' he accused.

'I was not sneaking! I saw it when you were showing me your new tractor, remember!' Heather's voice was a blend of sulkiness and outrage.

Their bickering acted on Ruth's raw nerves like an abrasive but she made herself bite back the sharp remonstrance that sprang to her lips. As the cupboard door was opened there came a clattering of toys on the floor and she was aware of Simon groping about among them. There followed a satisfied 'Hurrah!' and the next moment the full beam of the torch was shining directly into Ruth's eyes.

'Simon!' she reproved him testily. 'Switch it off at once! You're blinding me.'

'The batteries are good, Mummy,' he commented superfluously as he directed the beam at the ceiling.

'Switch it off, Simon, please,' she repeated. Her eyes, having become accustomed to the gloom, were now over-sensitive to the light. 'Simon!' Her voice hardened when he did not immediately obey. 'Simon, I told you to switch off the torch!' Her patience cracked. 'Why don't you do as I tell you?'

'I was only looking for my slippers,' he argued mutinously.

Paradoxically the mounting testiness in Ruth's voice seemed to ease the children's disquiet. Their mother's anger, though daunting, they nevertheless found strangely comforting; a thread of decisiveness weaving itself through a bewilderment of dread. Even Susan's desultory wailing was hushed.

'We're ready to go downstairs now,' Ruth said. 'You go first with the torch,' she instructed Simon. Carrying Susan and with Heather still holding on to her dressing gown she shuffled her way downstairs. As soon as they opened the kitchen door, Tansy leaped at them dementedly. 'Down, Tansy! Down!' The danger of being knocked over while holding Susan made Ruth's voice unnaturally stern and Simon, spurred by her anger, hit the dog with his torch. 'Don't do that!' she scolded him. 'You might break the torch.' Something deep inside her cringed with remorse that her first thought had been of damaging the torch rather than injuring their much-loved pet. But the moment was too critical for self reproach.

'You shouldn't be cruel to Tansy just because you're scared,' Heather immediately began chiding Simon, who responded with snappy resentment.

'Oh, do shut up the pair of you,' Ruth admonished them sharply. 'It doesn't help me to have to listen to you two squabbling.' She put Susan down in one of the armchairs. Heather quickly seated herself beside Susan sliding an arm around her as they huddled together against its soft cushioned back. Tansy, still panting distractedly, somehow managed to insert herself between them, and Heather, trying to placate her own alarm as well as Tansy's, put her hand on the dog's head and murmured endearments into the soft, warm ears.

With her thoughts still whirling in confusion Ruth tried to figure out what should be her next move. She tried flicking the light switches and when there was no result she took Simon's torch and checked to see that it was not their own fuses which had blown. Switching on the portable radio she turned the knobs agitatedly only to produce a faint cacophony of unintelligible voices interrupted by rattles of static. Hopefully she left it tuned in to their local station and lifted the telephone receiver. Despite there being no dialling tone she dialled the number of the police station. The only response was a sporadic clicking. She next tried dialling the operator and again there was no response. As a last resort she tried dialling 999 but her telephone appeared to be quite dead. With limp, hopeless fingers she replaced the receiver and, aware of the mutely questioning eyes of the children, tried desperately to disguise her worry. What should she do now, she debated. What could she do? But her mind was so tightened by stress it would not come up with a solution. How could she find out what was happening? Except for the coastguard's house across the road she had no immediate neighbours and, since she could not leave the children while she sought to find someone who could enlighten her, and since she could not risk taking them outdoors, it seemed her only recourse was to wait and pray hard for someone – anyone – to contact her. How long must she wait? Her dilemma hammered itself into her brain until she felt as if her head was trying to burst out of a too tight bandage.

With the aid of Simon's torch she rummaged in a drawer and found a short length of red candle, the remains of one which had decorated the Christmas table. She found matches and after lighting the candle she dribbled wax into a scallop shell that did duty as an ashtray and stood the candle in it. As its light wavered into the room, gilding the gloom, the eyes of the children fixed themselves on it as if mesmerized by the flickering flame.

'It's not Christmas!' Susan observed, with a childish attempt at derision.

'We know that, silly!' Heather's voice was scathing. 'How can it be Christmas when it's the day after your birthday?'

Thankful that the children were able to subordinate their terror long enough to indulge in a bout of mild taunting, Ruth seized the opportunity to say, 'Children, I must get myself dressed. Just please stay exactly where you are while I nip very quickly upstairs to get our clothes. No, don't follow me,' she coaxed, as they began to stir uneasily. 'I'll just grab some clothes quickly and I'll come down here to get dressed. I won't be a moment.' Impelled by the dread of leaving them alone for a moment longer than was necessary she leaped the stairs two at a time. When she re-entered the kitchen the children were still sitting, rigid with fear, their silence betraying that their ears had been tracking her every movement. Ruth put the clothes she was carrying on the kitchen table. 'There now,' she told them. 'Simon and Heather, get dressed as quickly as you can, and then Heather can help Susan dress while I put on the kettle.' Hastily she pulled on a pair of jeans and a T-shirt before lifting the bolster of the cooker, and while she was waiting for the kettle to boil she went over to the window and pulled aside the curtain. 'Dear God!' Her startled exclamation brought Simon and Heather running to look.

'There's a lot more fires now,' Simon observed. 'D'you think they've been started by bombs, Mummy?' Television had familiarized the children with the effects of bombing.

Ruth's eyes were riveted on the soaring and swirling expanse of flame that appeared to envelop a large area of the Port. She wondered how she should answer him. 'No, I still think it's more likely to have started with a flash of lightning,' she told him, and hoped her voice carried more conviction than she felt.

'But they must have spread, mustn't they?' Simon stated.

'They won't let them spread here to The Braes, will they, Mummy?' Heather questioned nervously.

'Oh no, darling. There's no risk of that happening.' Of that at least Ruth could be certain since The Braes stood on the side of the hill overlooking, yet well separated from, the compaction of buildings which comprised the actual Port. She turned away from the window, appalled by the sight of the sweeping tide of flame over which torrents of sparks merged with the thick black smoke. There had been other fires too, smaller ones which seemed to be sprouting haphazardly, like garden bonfires, among the houses. Had these been the result of sparks falling on highly combustible objects? Or was it possible they were incendiary bombs? She had never seen an incendiary bomb used, except on television news pictures, so she could only guess their efficacy. Dear God! her mind prayed silently. What is happening to the Port?

When she had given the children their warm drinks, she sat on a stool beside them close enough to give comfort if more sinister happenings impended, and as she sipped her own drink she tried to compose her thoughts sufficiently to produce a balanced explanation of the frightening disturbances of the night.

That they were connected in some way with the

general strike on the mainland she was becoming increasingly certain. With ships and airports having been brought to a standstill, postal deliveries, national newspapers and even telephone communications between the island and the mainland had virtually ceased. TV screens had become at first blurred and then completely blank and, save for programmes broadcast by the island's own small station, there had been no predictable radio contact. But the lack of news had not muffled reports of violent clashes between strikers and police; of lawless hordes of militants and thugs bent on systematic destruction; of armed insurrection and of racial rioting on a spreading scale; of prisoners escaping as a result of dwindling security in the gaols; and, most recently, of the necessary intervention of the armed forces.

The islanders, always ready to believe that mainland news was likely to be full of exaggerations, had at last begun to receive the reports with mounting concern, but their concern was for the fate of relatives and friends on the mainland rather than an expectation of becoming involved. The island's independent status, coupled with its distance from the mainland and with their assumption that only military and industrial targets would be the likely objectives for attack, had long habituated them to a belief in the safety of their neutrality. The island's economy was based almost exclusively on tourism, fishing and agriculture, and latterly, finance. It maintained no armed forces of its own and, apart from an offshore bombing range used for the training of USA and UK aircrews, a large abandoned airfield used periodically by the forces for instruction in target practice, and enviable deep-water harbours which could accommodate naval vessels paying courtesy visits, they had no significant connection with the military. Though there had been of late a noticeable increase in the use of the bombing range and more regular evidence of firing near the old airfield, the islanders had connected it only with far distant hostilities. The eventuality of the island itself ever becoming a target for bombardment had always seemed too improbable even for conjecture. Now, as Ruth ranged over the possibilities, questions pummelled at her mind. Could they have been living in a Fool's Paradise? Could such a wild improbability have become a reality? The idea struck her chillingly. If it were so, to what extent were she and the children in danger as a consequence? How could she find out?

A sudden whistling screech followed by a blasting crunch threw her off her stool and sent her reeling helplessly against the table. 'Cover your ears!' she yelled at the children and lunged forward to push them under the table and throw herself protectively over them. The house rocked and rattled about them, and as the floor heaved she was sure she heard the sound of shattering glass before yet another crunch shot her ears with a dull pain. A dizzy deafness engulfed her and, as she cowered beneath the table, positive that another blast would bring the house down and bury them, she tried to gather the screaming children closer to one another and to herself, striving to shield them from harm with her own slight body. Her hearing rushed back, to be rent by a confusion of hysterical squeals from the children mingled with the frenzied yelping of Tansy, who was scratching at the linoleum of the floor in a vain attempt to burrow beneath the heavy armchair. Ruth called to the dog, but Tansy was too distraught to pay heed and continued, ever more frantically, to squirm herself into the inch or so of possible sanctuary beneath the chair.

The noise of the blasts ebbed away into a brittle silence, and as she and the children lay, imprisoned by dread, she could feel the tautness of their bodies beneath her own. There was a simultaneous jump of alarm as the silence was riven by a heavy thumping on the outside door. Ruth tried to extricate herself but the children clung to her, preventing her from rising. The thumping became heavier and was accompanied by a muffled but insistent shouting. Persuading the children to release her, she struggled out from under the table but just as she was on her feet Simon grasped her ankle.

'Don't answer it, Mummy!' he cried out, and in the dim light she could see his young face distorted by extreme terror. 'Don't, Mummy! Don't! It might be a demon from outer space!'

Ruth hesitated, so dazed by events it took a second for her mind to reject the bizarre possibility. 'No, Simon!' she gasped. 'It'll be someone come to help us, I'm sure.' She was by no means sure of anything, but with a resolute shake of her head she nerved herself to go and open the door.

3

The coastguard from the headland station stepped into the room, closing the door behind him. 'You all okay, love?' He spoke with sharp concern. A widower with no family of his own, Uncle Guardy as the children called him was a favourite visitor at The Braes.

'Thank God you've come!' Ruth's body sagged with such an immensity of relief she almost fell against him. Tears filled her eyes but he managed only to spare her a compassionate glance before the children were beside them, the two younger ones begging his protection. Lifting one in each muscular arm, he held them close. 'No damage?' he enquired as his eyes searched the room. Noticing the kettle blowing clouds of steam he nodded to Ruth to lift it off the hotplate.

'I don't know. . . . I thought the house was coming down on top of us. . . . The windows must be broken. . . .' She pulled aside a curtain and her voice quavered into incredulity when she saw the windows were still intact. There followed another moment of disbelief when she realized the candle was still burning. She had felt the house shake on its foundations! She had felt the rush of the blast! And had she not heard the noise of breaking glass? Yet as she looked about her everything was exactly as it had been. Bewilderedly, she said, 'I'm positive I heard the sound of glass shattering. And the curtains flew out into the room. . . .' Her voice petered out as she looked up at him.

'It's a sort of shock wave,' the coastguard told her. 'They can sound as close as a direct hit.'

'Direct hit? But what's happening?' Ruth faltered.

'Those fires and then the church bell? The maroons? And there's no telephone and no radio. Something dreadful must be happening but I don't know what it all means. I don't know. . . .' Her voice rose and she pressed her hands to her cheeks as if trying to stem her questioning.

Above the heads of the children he regarded her steadily. 'We're under attack,' he informed her. 'And what it all means is that you and the kids have got to get out of here pretty quick,' he added.

For a moment she stared at him in blank incomprehension. 'Attack? From whom?' she echoed stupidly. 'And where can we go?

'Anywhere away from the Port.' His tone was emphatic. 'Get out into the country. Your sister-in-law's place will do, I reckon. But you've got no time to waste. Just grab a few necessities and get going.'

Ruth tried to move but her jumping nerves had sapped her strength. She could only stand staring at him, slowly shaking her head as though she had been knocked senseless by his words.

'Come on!' he insisted. 'Take whatever you might want. And be smart about it.' He set the two younger children down and kneeling beside Susan started to fasten the buckles of her sandals without noticing that she had them on the wrong feet. Ruth saw but felt too limp to intervene. To her the situation was still too grotesquely unreal for her to grasp. The coastguard looked up. 'Move, girl! Move!' He was shouting at her now. 'Or d'you want to stay here and risk your children being blasted to Kingdom come?'

Hardly knowing what she was doing she opened the fridge and began hastily stuffing the contents into an assortment of plastic bags.

'Where are we going, Mummy?' Susan asked.

'To Aunty Jeannie's,' Ruth replied with a kind of numbed abstraction.

'How long are we going to stay with Aunty Jeannie?' persisted Susan.

'I don't know.' Ruth continued tumbling whatever she could find in the way of food into bags, while Susan watched uncertainly and Simon and Heather darted to and fro collecting clothes and shoes and treasured possessions, too preoccupied to bandy more than the occasional monosyllable save when they collided with each other in their hurry.

'Suitcases?' The coastguard threw the question at Ruth while his hand was on the door into the hallway.

'The lumber room,' she told him.

'Blankets?' His voice came from the landing.

'My sister-in-law has plenty of blankets,' she called dismissively, but when he came downstairs Ruth noted he was carrying a bundle of blankets as well as two suitcases. Without commenting she turned her attention to pulling freshly laundered clothes from the cupboard and stuffing them into the suitcases. The coastguard let the blankets fall on the kitchen table. He cleared his throat before beginning in a bleak voice, 'Those first big blasts were boats loaded with explosives being rammed into the jetty. Just out of the blue they came!' he explained. 'It turns out there were a good few subversives on the island as well as trained anarchists and thugs. They've been lying low, some of them masquerading as tourists and others as conference delegates, but all of them ready for action the minute they got the signal from their bosses on the mainland.' He looked at her combatively, knowing she shrank from accepting the truth he was telling her. 'I know it's hard to believe, love. We never thought of such a thing happening here, but it's always been possible for it to happen and now it has.' He saw her dumb questioning and tapped the small VHF receiver in his pocket. 'It's quite true. I got it over my radio. They put the radio station out of action early on. Then they took over the

31

arms dump at the old airport. That was easy enough; the last regiment left on Friday and the next one wasn't due until this day week. Maybe there were guards,' he shrugged. 'I wouldn't know, but they'd soon loaded trucks with ammo and run them down to the Port to get as close as they could to the oil storage tanks and the gasworks. The police say there's carnage down there and they're trying to get people out as fast as they can. I reckon that last one was the gasworks. God only knows where their next target will be.'

Ruth's hand went nervously to her throat. Arms dump? At the old airfield? But hadn't it been only blank ammunition kept at the airfield? They had always believed so. She wanted to cry out her condemnation even while she recognized the futility of doing so. Her voice cracked as she asked, 'Wouldn't we be in less danger here rather than venturing out there?'

The coastguard's expression was unyielding. 'I reckon you'll be safer away from here,' he advised. 'The UK forces will counterattack any moment and you could get caught between the two,' he added warningly.

Between breaths of panic Ruth cried out, 'But why here? What could they gain by attacking the island? Why? Why?'

'The police suspect they've been secreting arms here for a longish while. Bringing them over on fishing boats and that sort of thing. They're never inspected. Why? you ask. They wouldn't do it without a good motive, would they?' Ruth was emptying another cupboard of the few packets and tins it contained. Today would have been her weekly shopping day. Today she'd hoped to be refilling the cupboard with packets of biscuits and crisps and other goodies to replace those consumed at Susan's birthday picnic. 'And why not the island?' the coastguard continued; 'When you come to think about it, the Port might be a good base for launching attacks

32

either way. And with no defences they'd reckon it would be easy enough to take it.' His voice dropped to a mutter. 'I reckon that's the way they must have been planning, anyway.' He indicated the suitcases. 'Those ready now?' he asked. Ruth knelt and closed the lids, snapping their fasteners firmly. 'Right!' he said. 'I'll stow these blankets in the car first and then come back for the cases.'

Ruth gestured with sudden despair. 'We can't get anywhere,' she told him. 'There's no petrol in the tank. I couldn't get any at either of the garages yesterday.'

'I'd thought of that,' he admitted. 'But we get a priority allowance and I can spare you enough to get you as far as your sister-in-law's place.'

She flashed him a grateful glance but almost instantly her despair returned. 'David,' she said. 'What will David do?' Her strained white face crumpled and she covered her eyes.

Putting down the blankets the coastguard took her firmly by the shoulders. '*Moonwind*'s still up north, isn't she?' he reminded her. 'David's well away from all this, love. He's better off than you and the children are likely to be if you try to stay on here.' She choked back her sobs as she tried to interrupt him but he went on, 'And he has Clyde with him, hasn't he?' Clyde, her cousin from America, was holidaying with them at The Braes and being a fisherman himself, had chosen to accompany David north on *Moonwind*. 'David and Clyde can be relied on to make a good job of looking after themselves and keeping out of trouble,' the coastguard summed up encouragingly.

'Yes, but how can I get a message to David?' she demanded. '*Moonwind* is due back shortly. David will be expecting to find us here.' Pulling a handkerchief from her sleeve, she blew her nose in an attempt to keep the sobs out of her voice.

'I'll get a signal to *Moonwind*,' the coastguard promised. Again he tapped his pocket. 'This thing transmits as well as receives, don't forget.'

'You'll be staying here?' she asked, surprised, realizing it had not occurred to her to wonder what he himself was going to do.

'Oh, I've got to stay, love.' There was a mingling of pride and resolution in his voice. 'There's no off duty for me when there's any emergency. Not that there'll be any off duty for any of us until this is sorted out,' he added.

Releasing his grip of her shoulders he again picked up the blankets.

'I must leave a note for David because he's bound to come back here,' Ruth insisted.

The coastguard repressed a testy sigh. 'Yes, you do that and if your house is still standing when David gets back he'll find your note.' He saw her wince as he spoke of the possible destruction of her home but compunction was over-ridden by anxiety. It seemed to him she had still not grasped the peril of the situation and was wasting precious time.

She was searching agitatedly for pen and paper when the dreaded whistling ripped into the night again seizing her with terror. She heard the coastguard shout and saw him with one swift movement thrust Susan under the table. As Simon and Heather leaped to join her, he and Ruth threw themselves over the children while three ear-splitting explosions followed one another in quick succession. The curtains billowed, the candle flickered as if in a fierce draught and, like an expected sequel, Susan's array of birthday cards fluttered with a sound like tiny sighs from the mantelpiece to the floor. The minutes went by as they waited in tight suspense for further explosions but outside the night settled. The coastguard shuffled to his feet. Ruth and the children followed more cautiously and as they

34

stood tremblingly together the stunned stillness was broken by a petulant wail from Susan.

'Those big bangs have made my birthday cards fall all over the floor,' she complained. As she broke away to collect them Ruth and the coastguard exchanged mutely incredulous glances. Susan pounced on her favourite card which had come from her Aunty Jeannie and which depicted a small girl wearing a pink tutu and poised on the pointes of pink ballet shoes. The card also bore a large figure 4 in gold and the greeting, also in gold, read: 'To my darling niece on her birthday.' She pressed the card to her breast. Susan had been promised a course of ballet lessons as soon as she was five, and already her dreams centred on the day when she too would be poised in a pink tutu exactly like the little girl on the card.

'There seems to be another lull so let's get going,' said the coastguard, picking up the blankets once more. 'Come on! Everybody carry something and follow me outside.'

'Here you are, children,' Ruth said, handing them various bags and bundles.

Simon hung back.

'Hurry please, Simon,' Ruth bade him.

'I think we ought to stay here until Daddy comes back,' he demurred. He was scowling heavily, a subterfuge he often used to check tears.

'Darling, we must go,' she tried to reason with him but her manner was short. 'You heard what Uncle Guardy said and after that last explosion I know he's right. It's not safe to stay. We must all go to Aunty Jeannie's and wait there for Daddy and Uncle Clyde to come.' She pressed a hand on his shoulder. 'Daddy wouldn't want us to stay anywhere we were in danger, would he?'

'But if Daddy comes here without knowing

35

anything's wrong he'll be in danger,' he maintained stubbornly.

'But he will know. Uncle Guardy's going to get a message to him.'

'Couldn't I stay with Uncle Guardy just to make sure Daddy does get a message?'

'No, Simon. You cannot. Please be sensible and don't make difficulties for me. Don't you think I have enough already? You know I won't go without you,' she added with increasing sternness. Lifting tearbright eyes to hers, he yielded with a compliant nod. 'Now will you carry this bag out to the car,' Ruth coaxed, handing him one of the carrier bags. 'It's pretty heavy,' she cautioned.

'I can carry a lot more than this, Mummy,' he claimed, picking up what was evidently a much heavier bag and testing it for weight. Satisfied, he collected his precious torch and with the bag pulling him down lopsidedly he hobbled out to the car. Without a word Heather valiantly picked up the bag spurned by her brother. 'Mummy can I sit in the passenger seat?' she asked.

'No! I want Simon beside me in the passenger seat,' Ruth insisted. Heather pouted but did not argue.

'Now, Susan, it's your turn. You can carry this bag, can't you? It's not too heavy.' Turning, Ruth held out a lightly packed bag towards the spot where Susan had been standing only a moment or two before. But Susan was no longer there. 'Susan!' yelled Ruth irritably. 'Susan!' she repeated peering about the shadowed kitchen. 'That child!' she ejaculated, running out to check whether Susan was already in the car. Susan had a natural propensity for elusiveness; for vanishing from the spot where everyone could have sworn they had seen her only seconds previously. After a period she was usually found in some secluded corner of the house or in one of the sheds engrossed in happy play with her family of dolls and totally oblivious of the fact that she was the object of search. When Ruth found Susan was not with the other children in the car, her anger, the anger of sheer panic – erupted. She ran back into the house. 'Susan!' her voice harshened. 'Susan, come here at once. This very minute.' There came the sound of scuffling footsteps on the stairs and an astonished Susan appeared in the kitchen doorway. 'You naughty girl!' Ruth berated her. 'You shouldn't have gone upstairs without saying anything to me.'

'I only went to get Gruntly Finny,' Susan explained guilelessly. 'He's frightened of the bangs.' She stood there hugging the teddy bear. 'An' I brought Heather's penguin too 'cos she'd left it on her bed an' she won't ever go to sleep without him.'

Relief and understanding melted Ruth's anger. 'All right, darling. Now perhaps you can take this bag out to the car for me and please, Susan, please stay there with Simon and Heather until I come. I shan't be long so I don't want you to come back into the house. Promise?'

Susan promised somewhat absently and without relinquishing either Gruntly Finny or Heather's penguin or even the precious birthday card to which she still clung she tried to pick up the bag her mother had indicated. It instantly slipped from her hand, spilling some of its contents.

'Oh, Susan!' Ruth tried hard to conceal her exasperation. 'For goodness' sake, put that card on the table and then you can hold the bag safely as well as holding Gruntly Finny and Penguin.' Sullenly, Susan did as she was told.

The coastguard, returning for the last of the parcels, took charge. 'All right now,' he said. 'Susan, you can come with me.' He looked at Ruth. 'You finish off what you want to do and then come as quickly as you can.'

Alone in the kitchen Ruth bent over the table, pen

in hand. Not troubling to look for notepaper she seized the treasured birthday card. 'Have taken children to Jeannie's. See you there. All our love. Ruth' she scribbled on the back of it. Taking the tea caddy from the mantelpiece she set it on the table, propped the card against it and, after a swift, dejected survey of the kitchen, went out into the paling dawn, slamming the door behind her.

The smell of smoke was rough in her nostrils and she threw only one short glance in the direction of the Port. The coastguard was holding open the door of the car.

'I've put the petrol in the tank and everything seems to be pretty well stowed,' he told her. 'Even Tansy,' he added, giving a wry nod to where Tansy had settled herself determinedly in Heather's lap. As soon as Ruth was seated he closed the door. 'Now take my advice,' he said. 'I'm not trying to fuss you but make sure you lock all the doors,' he reminded her as she got in.

'Oh, that's all right,' she told him, thinking he was cautioning her on account of the children. 'There are safety locks on the rear doors.'

'Lock all of them,' he insisted. As she leaned over and obediently snapped down the locks, he added, 'And don't use your headlights at all. Now remember what I'm saying,' he went on as he saw her raised eyebrows. 'Don't stop for anything or anybody, not unless you're forced to.' He spoke so positively that for a moment she wondered if he was overplaying the danger. 'You might think you're okay, but I saw some of this sort of thing during the last war and it taught me the only safe way to get anywhere is to keep moving. Keep your foot as hard down on that accelerator as you can manage safely and remember if you get in a mess it's every man for himself. Don't forget your first thought's got to be for the safety of the children.'

'I wish you'd come with us, Uncle Guardy,' Heather said imploringly.

'I'm afraid I can't do that, my darling,' he told her and immediately needed to clear the hoarseness from his voice. 'Goodbye for now, children. I'm sure you'll all be back home again soon.' His grim mouth relaxed into a contrived smile as he stood back and raised a hand in salute. Wanly the children attempted to salute in return.

Ruth held out her hand. 'Goodbye,' she said brokenly. 'God bless you and keep you safe. And thank you for everything.' She was crying unashamedly now, letting the tears flow unheeded down her cheeks. 'You will keep a look-out for David, won't you?'

She saw a glint of something like reproof in his eyes and wished she had not thought it necessary to remind him.

'You can count on that, girl,' he promised.

She let in the clutch and as the car surged forward her last impression was of his sadly bereft expression as he stood, still saluting the energetic waving of the children.

In the kitchen of The Braes the stump of red candle which Ruth in her agitation had neglected to dout, burned on, its dwindling flame illuminating the gold lettering on Susan's birthday card and sliding lissome shadows across the figure of the dancer. The candle guttered and finally died, leaving only a crusted pool of wax in the bottom of the scallop shell.

Again the curtains billowed.

4

As soon as the car turned into the main road they saw ahead of them and behind them hurrying shapes patterning the half light. So many people! People striding along with heavy haversacks on their backs; people hustling along carrying bulging bags and baskets; people pushing perambulators and loaded bicycles; people plodding; people carrying or dragging young children. Just like refugees. The thought flashed across Ruth's mind as she recalled TV and newspaper coverage of similar scenes in different parts of the world. Refugees! At first the impact of the word was so dumbfounding that her mind baulked at accepting it. Could this really be happening here on their own island? Were she and the children now refugees? As the grim word embedded itself dismally into Ruth's consciousness she knew that indeed they were all fugitives fleeing from a peril which, without warning, had shattered overnight the serenity of their small world. But she and the children must count themselves luckier than most. Thanks to the coastguard they had transport and they had a haven to go to.

Her eyes strayed from the road to the pink-tinged hills for which they were making and she experienced a renewed whiplash of panic before she realized that the pinkness was not the distant glare of flames reflected in the sky but only the first flush of an incipient dawn.

'Red sky at night, sailor's delight.
Red sky at morning, sailor's warning.'

Instantly her concern shifted to her husband. Dear

God, don't let it be stormy, she prayed. Please bring us all safely together again! She tried to ponder on what David might be doing at this moment. He would be up and about, she was sure, using every vestige even of half light to prepare *Moonwind* for sailing tomorrow at high tide. Provided there were no hold-ups and given good weather then he and Clyde could arrive by the week-end. Dear, dear God! Please give them fair weather! Conjecture was intermingled with impassioned prayer until the car jolted with the force of yet another explosion. The children cried out and, as she struggled to conceal the extent of her own terror, conjecture was routed by the prayers that coursed ceaselessly through her mind.

A low lingering haze, like a shawl shrugged off from the shoulders of the hills, was delaying the promised dawn and as Ruth drove on, using only sidelights as the coastguard had directed, she tried not to heed the raised arms and entreating gestures of the walkers among whom she had to manoeuvre the car. Though she was angered and sickened by their plight and distressed at her own inability to offer help, she was at the same time relieved that the dim light made recognition difficult. Many of these people would be acquaintances; some could be friends; some schoolmates of her own children. Her self-torment was checked by an aggressive horn tooting as a car came quickly up behind her and passed at speed, scattering pedestrians and forcing her almost into the bank at the roadside. 'Yobbos!' she screamed after them, unleashing a token of her rage on the occupants. At the rate it was travelling it could quite easily have knocked down some of the people; perhaps have maimed or even killed them! Ruth seethed, but along with indignation came the horrendous suspicion that perhaps, as the coastguard had hinted, there had already been so much maiming and killing down in the Port that those who had witnessed it had become indifferent to every feeling save the urgency to escape. Even as she shuddered the thought away Ruth saw her opportunity, and taking advantage of the temporarily cleared road she trod hard down on the accelerator. She must steel herself to forego pity. For her children's sake she must press on.

Suddenly there was a blinding flash, a deafening crump and the car lifted as if she had driven too fast over a hump in the road. For a second her body felt as if it had been squeezed hard and then quickly jerked free, leaving her spine feeling as if it was trying to push through the top of her head. She was conscious of the children squealing; she had the sensation that she was screaming too. But she did not stop the car. Her hands were gripping the steering wheel, her foot was on the accelerator, but now it was terror driving; a new dimension in terror that made a mockery of all earlier terrors. The car was speeding recklessly; speeding away from the thick cloud of smoke that looked as if it was pursuing them; speeding away from whatever was happening behind the smoke.

The continuous screaming of the children forced her eventually to take a grip of herself, and becoming aware of her own rapid breathing and trembling limbs she slowed the car almost to a crawl while she checked none of them was injured. Thank God! Not only had she and the children come through unscathed but, judging from its performance, the car also appeared to have suffered no damage. Acknowledging their lucky escape she released her breath in a long shuddering sigh.

The children's screaming had now subsided to distressed whimperings mingled with a timorous chorus of 'Mummy! Mummy!' from the two younger ones, and she longed to stop the car and hug them. Resisting the longing was like having her arms strongly manacled.

She desperately wanted to hold them close – a fierce surge of mother love making it seem possible that by holding them thus she could draw their fear into her own body as a poultice draws out poison from a wound. But she had to resist. She had to resist also the impulse to look back along the road in case she was assailed by a compulsion to return and do what she could to help. Dear God! Her lips moved soundlessly. Don't let anyone blame me! Recalling her own condemnation of the 'yobbos' who had raced their vehicle without regard for the refugees she was wrung with an agony of guilt. But her mouh stayed grimly set. She drove on, her eyes fixed on the road ahead as she murmured automatic reassurances to the children that they were now out of danger.

When they had travelled some distance further Heather shouted, 'Look, Mummy! There's a lady in front of us and she's carrying a little baby. Please, Mummy, couldn't we give them a lift in our car?' she pleaded.

Ruth changed down. There would, she knew, be room for another person in the car and here, where no other refugees were in sight, surely it would be safe to stop? Surely, no matter how dire the situation, she could not leave the woman to struggle on with a small child? Here was an opportunity not only to salve her own anguished conscience, but to demonstrate to the children that she was not so callous as to refuse help when she could do so without exposing them to danger. One of her torments had been to have them witness her apparent disregard for the plight of others.

Hearing the car, the woman stopped and waited, dispiritedly shifting the fretful child against her shoulder. Ruth pulled up and wound her window partly down.

'We can squeeze you and the baby in,' she called. 'We shall have to move things round a bit first though.'

The woman stared at her sullenly without speaking. Tired out probably, Ruth surmised and wondered fleetingly how she had managed to outdistance all the other walkers. Her voice took on a more compassionate tone. 'I'm just going to drive on to that lay-by,' she explained. 'There's room there for us to stop and sort ourselves out.'

The woman's expression became suddenly venomous and pulling at the handle of the door she shrieked 'Bill! Bill!' Immediately a man leaped out from behind the bank and brandished a large stick.

'Get out you lot!' he commanded threateningly. Pushing the woman aside he grasped the door handle and wrenched at it. When it did not yield he began thrashing the stick against the roof of the car and Ruth, fearing he was about to smash the windows, yelled at the children to lie down. She had not stopped the engine but in her haste to get away she stalled the car. The man snarled a stream of filthy abuse. 'Get out!' he repeated savagely. 'We're having this car. You can bloody well start walking.' His hand was on the half-open window, weighing against her desperate eforts to close it. The next moment he had thrust the stick into the car and through the steering wheel, pinning her back against the seat. His hand reached for the lock. Simon now jumped up and, leaning across his mother struck at the man's hand with his torch, but the man only cursed him and brought his arm round to weigh more heavily on the window while his hand reached again for the lock. With all his strength Simon pulled at the stick trying to make the man release it, and at the same time Ruth tried to seize the groping fingers and bend them back in a manner which she recalled was reputed to be an effective way of foiling the clutch of an assailant. But the man's fingers were like strong steel springs. They were on the lock. It was at that precise moment that Susan's terror caused her to press

44

Gruntly Finny even more tightly to her chest. At the bear's resulting grunt, Tansy, who since the last explosion had been a cowering bundle behind the children, launched herself over the front seat and with a series of outraged snarls and yelps snapped viciously at the man's hand. The suddenness of the dog's attack caught him unawares and with an oath he recoiled, shaking his bleeding fingers and releasing his hold of the stick. Ruth was quick to seize her chance. As Simon jerked the man's stick into the car she wound up the window, started the engine, rammed in the gear and got the car into motion. Unprepared, the man lurched back against the woman, knocking her and the child against the bank. Recovering, he lunged at the rear of the car as if he was intent on holding the bumper, but he was too late. The car was pulling away too strongly and he was left shouting and gesticulating at the roadside.

Simon drew the stick triumphantly beside him as if he was retrieving a trophy. 'We'll keep this here, Mummy,' he said. 'In case we meet any more bad men.'

'Are we safe from that man now, Mummy?' Heather asked.

Ruth's mouth was too dry to answer and she could only nod. The incident had so weakened her she had to concentrate on keeping her grip of the wheel.

The children were soon exclaiming over their experience with a competitive indignation that seemed to have blunted the sharp edges of their fear. But Ruth's heart was still hammering; her stomach was still knotted with fear. How unnerving the encounter had been! How nauseating! How narrow an escape they'd had! If the woman had delayed calling to the man until they had reached the lay-by, and the doors had been opened as she'd intended then, it would certainly have been impossible for them to fight off the attack. Thank God the coastguard had insisted she lock all the car

45

doors, she thought, as she endeavoured to overcome her churning stomach.

'I do wish Daddy was with us,' moaned Susan. 'He wouldn't have let that bad man frighten us.'

'We all wish that, don't we, Mummy?' Simon's glance was full of appeal. 'Don't cry, Mummy,' he pleaded, seeing the tears seeping at the corners of her eyes.

Looking down at him she saw his own eyes were brimming. 'I'm trying not to, Simon,' she managed to say. 'But what's just happened was so horrible I can't really stop myself.'

'Tansy was a very brave dog, wasn't she?' Heather pointed out. 'She soon bit that nasty man when Gruntly Finny made a noise. She made him bleed. I saw the blood,' she added gloatingly.

'Gruntly Finny made a noise because I told him to,' claimed Susan. 'It was Gruntly who made Tansy bite him.'

'Tansy was truly heroic,' Ruth admitted. 'We owe her a great deal for scaring that man away. He would have taken the car and everything in it except ourselves and we would have had to walk all the way to Aunt Jeannie's. And wasn't Susan clever to make Gruntly Finny grunt just at that very moment? I wish I could give you a big hug and a kiss for that,' she added. 'I will when we stop.'

'I'll give her a big hug and a kiss for you,' said Heather and promptly did so.

'I'll give you a kiss too when we stop,' promised Simon.

'Tansy's going to have a big hug and a kiss too, aren't you, Tansy?' Heather said, fussing and crooning over Tansy who, apparently regarding her intervention as proof of her loyalty, had retreated as swiftly as she had attacked and was once more ensconced on Heather's lap.

When she considered she had achieved a sufficient measure of calm, Ruth said, 'Children, what happened back there is something I cannot take the risk of having happen again. You do understand, don't you? I mustn't stop for anyone again no matter how sorry we might feel for them. You do understand?' she repeated. 'So please don't ask me to, will you? Even if it's someone we know, or think we know.'

'I promise I won't,' affirmed Simon, and Heather and Susan echoed his promise.

'I don't like to seem cruel any more than you would,' Ruth explained, as if she had to justify her behaviour to herself as well as the children.

'That man was cruel,' asserted Heather. 'When I looked back I saw him punching the woman, and the baby was lying on the ground.' Her tone was one of distress. 'I do wish we could have brought just the little baby with us,' she added.

'Well, I've got the man's stick,' proclaimed Simon as if he regarded it as an acceptable substitute. 'And I'm going to keep it.'

Continuing to stare fixedly ahead Ruth was at the same time wrestling with an almost overwhelming desire to stop the car, lay her head on the steering wheel and indulge in self-recriminatory grief. The hurt of her own conduct, necessary as it had been under the circumstances, persisted in stinging her overwrought nerves, and as her mind retraced the incident again and again she questioned whether she had needed to be so pitiless. The man's behaviour had been monstrous but could she not perhaps have bargained with him to allow the woman and child or at least the child to be helped on the way to safety? But she'd had no option, had she? The way the man had behaved, it had to be them or us. The image of the child pecked at her memory like a predatory beak at a kill, making her wince even as it reinforced the fierce protectiveness she felt for her own children.

With difficulty she wrenched her thoughts from what had passed and tried to concentrate on ensuring their future safety. The dread of further explosions was a constant agony but there was a secondary dread that a small mishap, perhaps a puncture, might force her to stop, thus laying them open to the risk of a similar incident to the one from which they had so narrowly escaped. She began for the first time to question the lack of traffic on the road. Admittedly few people would have had petrol for private cars but she had expected to see other vehicles. Was she a forerunner or a tail-ender in this trail to safety? She started to chide herself for being stupidly slow in getting the children away. She started to worry that the lack of traffic might mean there was danger ahead — or about to overtake them. She wondered whether she was right to continue along the main road; whether by doing so she was subjecting them all to further hazard. It was imperative they get to her sister-in-law's by the quickest possible route but might not a by-road prove a surer way? If only there was someone to advise her!

'That explosion that nearly lifted the car off the road must have done a lot of damage,' said Simon as if his thoughts had been running along the same lines as her own. 'Maybe the road was blown up.'

Horror again snatched at Ruth. Was it possible their car had been the last to get through? The suspicion crept through her chillingly. Had they been only a few minutes later, would they too have been trapped by the destruction? Her thoughts sheered away from the subject.

The morning mist had now lifted and the sun was slipping errant shafts of silvery light over the road. Out of the sunlight two motor cyclists in military uniform approached them.

They watched first with interest which turned to apprehension as the first motor cyclist circled round them, signalling them to stop. When they had stopped the second motor cyclist drew up beside them.

'Pull right in to the side of the road,' he commanded. He lifted his goggles. 'We have tanks on the way and they need all the road. How d'you come to be here, anyway?' His manner was brisk and officious. Hurrying to comply with his direction Ruth ran the car as close as she could to the bank. The man nodded perfunctory approval. 'After the tanks have gone you must take the first side road you come to. We can't have you blocking this road. You must keep off the main road altogether. That's an order. Got it?' His steely blue eyes flicked over the car and its occupants before he pulled down his goggles and revved his engine.

Ruth wanted desperately to ask what was happening but before she had a chance to frame the question he was gone.

'Were they our soldiers, Mummy?' Heather asked.

'I think so,' Ruth said unsteadily. A second later she added with more confidence, 'Yes, I'm sure they must have been.'

They sat stiff and silent as if trapped in the car as they listened and waited for whatever was to happen. The noise of the departing motor bikes had barely died away when the road seemed to begin vibrating, and within minutes a line of tanks was rolling towards them with such blind, undeviating menace that it looked for a few seconds as if they were intent on crushing the car and its occupants like a tin can under a roller. Dust swirled about the dry road and the smell of hot fuel seeped into the car. The children cringed visibly and Ruth tried to think of some trivial remark which might even fractionally ease the tension but it was Heather who, as soon as the last tank had ground its way past, announced complacently; 'Well they should soon be able to kill all the bad men.' The other two children seemed to be equally comforted by the prospect. 'I wonder where they got the tanks from?' Heather went on to query.

'The army could have flown them in in no time,' asserted Simon.

'Do they keep men inside those tanks?' Susan wanted to know.

'Of course there are soldiers in them now, silly. I've got a picture in one of my books at home that shows what they're like inside. I wish I'd brought it with me,' Simon lamented.

'Would you like to try driving one, Simon?' Heather enquired. 'When you're grown up I mean?'

As they fell to discussing the things they planned to do in the future Ruth, envying their unfledged emotions which could so easily shift from trepidation to near nonchalance, only half listened to their chatter. Temporarily disencumbered from the necessity of being ready with comforting assurances she was able to give her whole attention to getting off the road as the soldier had instructed. Spotting a T-junction which led in the direction she wanted to go, she turned into it thankfully and found herself in a narrow, unfamiliar lane bordered by high thorn hedges which she assumed were the boundaries of farm fields. A little further on there were a few scattered cottages, holiday homes, judging from their deserted appearance, awaiting the arrival of summer visitors. Now and then she glimpsed a farm-house and buildings but since they were set well back from the road it was impossible for her to tell whether or not they were still occupied.

She had driven more than a mile along the lane before she espied a human figure – an old man leaning on a gate and fondling the nose of a gentle old work-horse. Beside him lay a shaggy collie dog, quiescent but watchful. The normality of the scene was so inspiriting that Ruth braked almost to a stop before she remembered she must keep her foot on the clutch in case of trickery. The old man turned to watch her.

'What's happened to everyone?' she called.

He gave the car and its occupants a lengthy glance of appraisal before replying. 'Gone!' he said. The collie barked once as if echoing the forlorn monosyllable.

'Because of what's happening?' She hadn't much doubt of his answer.

He nodded slowly. 'You can't blame them,' he said.

'Why not you?' she asked.

He hauled himself away from the gate as if to demonstrate his arthritic limbs and bent back. 'I don't reckon we'd get far,' he said cynically. 'I've been offered a lift but I wouldn't want to leave the old dog and the horse. We've been together too long for that.' There was a stick leaning against the gate and grasping it the old man came hobbling towards the car. With a quiver of uneasiness Ruth shifted her foot from the brake. Her trust had been too badly mauled for her to allow even a crippled old man to get too close to the car. When he paused she did not know whether it was because he had sensed her unease or because he needed a respite from the labour of hauling his stiff limbs along.

'You've come from the Port?' he asked.

'From just this side,' she told him.

'You were lucky to get out, from what I've heard.' He indicated the car. 'They were saying others haven't been so lucky.' Ruth nodded gravely. He bowed his head. 'I suppose you can say I've been lucky to be left alive, though what's life to someone of my age when you've not got a home?' Ruth looked at him with compassionate enquiry. 'Some mad louts came last night and when they'd scoffed or destroyed every bit of food in the house they piled the furniture in the middle of the kitchen and set fire to it. Then they went off laughing and shouting.' Ruth's eyes widened in horror. 'Dear God Almighty but I'm glad my old woman is not alive this day to see what they've done to our home. They even burned the bed she died in,' he repined as if that had been the crowning sacrilege. His moist old eyes looked into Ruth's.

'Who are they? Who was responsible?' Her voice was harsh with impotent rage.

'Why these thugs that are swarming over the island. Wherever they've come from nobody seems to know, but they've taken to looting and burning, aye and some say killing when they couldn't get what they wanted any other way,' he replied. 'I was out at the back when they came to my house and I heard all this shouting and brawling so I kept out of the way. When they'd gone it was too late to do anything.'

'They must be insane!' Ruth whispered incredulously. She wished she could offer to help him but she knew there was nothing she could do that would not put their own chances of safety in jeopardy.

He pulled a crumpled khaki handkerchief from his pocket and wiped his eyes. 'You take my advice, Missus, and get on to where you're going. You don't want to meet up with any of these mad gangs. I reckon they're drugged to the eyeballs and don't know the half of what they're doing.'

His words acted as a spur and she let in the clutch. 'Goodbye,' she called. 'I hope you'll get help soon. Let's pray things will soon be back to normal.' Even to her the words sounded banal but she could think of nothing more constructive to say.

'I daresay we'll be all right,' he called back. 'We've still got Prince's stable for shelter.' He raised a listless arm in a gesture of farewell and then limped back to the gate to resume his communion with the horse.

5

The old man's story had added yet another facet to Ruth's trepidation and there niggled at her mind the disturbing possibility that Jeannie may not have been as untouched by events as Ruth had imagined she would be. Would they arrive at the smallholding only to discover Jeannie was herself preparing to leave? Would she have already left? Her thoughts, lurching from question to question, were pursued by an urge of common sense that told her to dismiss her doubts as being over-reaction to a surfeit of fear. Jeanie's smallholding was tucked so discreetly into a secluded valley among the hills that it was highly improbable even a wandering maurauder would stumble across it. Once there she and the children would be safe and secure from molestation and the fear of fire and explosions. And soon David and Clyde would be with them and their stay would no doubt develop into the sort of holiday they had so often enjoyed at the smallholding. Jeannie would be only too delighted to have their company. Ruth suspected she would not be averse to having Clyde's company either. Since her cousin and her husband's sister had first met she had noticed a growing attraction between them, an attraction which she was certain accounted for Clyde prolonging his stay on the island.

After indignant comments on the old man's experiences and condemnation of the perpetrators the two girls had gone quiet and glancing in her driving mirror Ruth saw they were slumped together and that they appeared to be fast asleep. Simon, sitting beside her, was staring with drowsy pensiveness at the road ahead but when she stole a second glance she met his wide-awake eyes. As if to prove his wakefulness he extracted a bag from his jacket pocket and offered her a jelly baby which she declined with an apologetic nod. She was in no way disposed to allow herself to relax her vigilance for a single instant. Indeed she would not allow herself to recognize even a symptom of tiredness, but the silence in the car gave her a welcome sense of privacy; an opportunity when she could, without interruption from the searching questions of the children, sort out the jumble of worries which fretted her.

The car was climbing steadily towards the hills having left all but the occasional farmstead well behind and it was now following the winding track which would eventually lead them to Jeannie's and safety. A fragment of relief snicked cosily among Ruth's worries, enabling her to sit less stiffly in her seat as she tried to calculate the distance they had still to cover.

Her reflections were broken into by the restless whining of Tansy and remembering the dog had not only foregone her morning outing but had since been cooped up in the car Ruth braked to a halt.

'Come on, Tansy,' she invited, opening the door and getting out as quietly as she could, and, while Tansy capered about alternately sniffing and relieving herself, Ruth stood by the car and for the first time since they had left looked back in the direction of the Port obscured now by a pall of black smoke which was slowly drifting out to sea. Her stomach contracted and her breath seemed to be scouring her throat as she tried to think what devastation the smoke concealed. With misting eyes she pictured The Braes. Shrinking from even speculating whether her home and all the dear, familiar things it comprised might now be no more than a heap of smouldering rubble she mused over how long it would be before they might be able to return. She recalled the happiness of Susan's birthday party. Was it really only yesterday they had felt so safe and protected? How inconceivable it would have seemed then had anyone suggested their world could grow so mad and brutish overnight! She shook her head in dismay, fighting against the longing to throw herself on the ground and cry aloud at the wickedness of it all.

Her gaze rested on the sea, slate grey in the morning light, and she again pondered how long it would be before David would come. Would *Moonwind* be diverted by the events of the night? Had the coastguard succeeded in getting a message through? But surmise was pointless, she realized. She had to accept that David would come just as quickly as he possibly could and meantime the best thing she could do was to get to Jeannie's and wait there for his arrival.

Her glance shifted to pick out the segments of the main road where they were visible. She identified the diversion she had taken and traced the wavering track which, like a length of perished rubber draped carelessly across the hillside, served to link the otherwise isolated farmsteads: The 'Milky Way' as the farmers had dubbed it since the track had been engineered primarily for the lorry which collected their milk churns.

She focused on a small cottage snuggled so deep into the hillside it looked as if it might be cowering away from the overbearing heights behind it. Some urban dweller's summer retreat from the madding crowd and doubtless as yet unoccupied, she assumed, until she saw a puff of smoke caught by an eddy of breeze and wafted into invisibility. A second puff followed and vanished similarly. Just getting up, she supposed and looking down at her wrist noticed for the first time that she had omitted to put on her watch. She looked back at the cottage. Her eyes narrowed and with a bound she was in the car and calling urgently to Tansy. Looting, burning, killing, the old man had said and Ruth, having grasped suddenly that the smoke she was seeing was coming not from the chimney but from the roof of the house, thrust the car into gear and raced on.

Heather woke to the slam of the door and instantly her face resumed its apprehensive expression.

'It's all right,' Ruth whispered. 'I stopped just to let Tansy out. She needed a little saunter.'

'It's taking us an awful long time to get to Aunty Jeannie's,' Heather said querulously.

'Well, we've had to go a lot longer way round, remember,' Simon informed her.

'Are you sure we're on the right road, Mummy?' Heather pursued. 'We haven't passed the shop yet, have we?'

'Yes, I'm quite sure,' Ruth told her. 'We don't pass the shop coming this way but it's the right road nevertheless. You'll be able to recognize where we are in just a few minutes.' And when, after a further half mile or so, she swung the car into a yet steeper track, changing down as the engine laboured, Heather, recognizing the road, murmured contentedly. Susan woke and since neither of the girls were disposed to go to sleep again they continued to chat desultorily at first, and then more animatedly as they got on to the subject of sleeping arrangements at the smallholding.

'Aunty Jeannie's got a tent,' Simon said. 'I know because she promised I could sleep in it next time I came.'

'I wish I could sleep in the tent,' said Heather wistfully. 'Mummy, d'you think Aunty Jeannie will let me sleep in the tent?'

'I don't know, darling. Don't pester, will you? We must just wait and see.'

The car breasted the shoulder of the hill and began the twisting descent towards what the children always referred to as 'The Secret Valley' where Jeannie's smallholding lay pinched between two humps of the hill. Ruth strained her eyes for signs of anything out of the ordinary, reminding herself as she did so that she had seen nothing to increase her worries since the smoke from the cottage roof and that, by this time, was a good way behind them.

'I can see Mr Biggs's farm!' sang out Heather. The Biggs were Jeannie's nearest neighbours, their farm being only a third of a mile from the smallholding though out of sight behind a rumple of hill. Ruth drove past slowly. The house itself was screened from the road by a thick rhododendron hedge but the solid stone outbuildings, looking as functionally unkempt as ever, were plainly visible. She scanned them keenly hoping to catch a sight of Mr Biggs or Lennie, his hired hand, going about the business of the day and perhaps to receive a friendly wave of recognition indicating that life here was uninterrupted by any backwash of conflict. She saw no movement until she caught sight of a large boar which was rooting its way along the grass-verged entrance towards the open gate. Its appearance served to slacken a morsel of her tension since she knew from past experience that the boar had a habit of escaping from its sty and that very soon it would be missed and someone would come in search of it. Almost as if she had caught a waft of it brewing she began to recognize her yearning for a cup of coffee.

'Here at last!' shouted Heather as they turned into the entrance of Jeannie's smallholding. 'Come on, Susan!'

'No, no. Not yet!' Ruth bade them. 'Now I want you to wait quietly in the car for a moment while I go and tell Aunty Jeannie what's happened and why we're here.' The children looked puzzled. 'She probably doesn't know what's been happening down at the Port,' she explained. Silencing the chorus of protests she got out of the car and called Tansy to follow her. A swift glance about her revealed that Jeannie's brake was still parked outside the garage. The house was quiet as she expected it to be and the detectable smell of the smokeless fuel stove hovered reassuringly in the still morning air. At the gate of their pen she saw that the poultry were clustered evidently awaiting their morning feed while a mother hen with her retinue of young chicks came cluckingly to investigate her arrival. Ruth, denying herself the luxury of pausing to absorb the peacefulness of it all, hurried on.

Like most of the residents in the remoter parts of the island Jeannie had always considered the locking of a door the over-cautious habit of town dwellers so Ruth was not surprised that the door opened when she lifted the latch. Stepping into the hallway she stood at the foot of the stairs and called Jeannie's name and when there was no response she called again. She frowned. Should she go upstairs and check if Jeannie was still asleep? Quashing a pin-prick of disquiet she told herself that of course Jeannie by this time would be out attending to the morning milking.

The necessity of keeping a constant eye on the car drove her outside again. 'All right,' she said, opening the doors to allow the children to scramble out. 'You can go inside now. I think Aunty Jeannie is probably out milking but we can go in and wait. Now don't make much noise just in case Aunty Jeannie is still sleeping.' Ruth made the behest as from habit, confessing to herself that she desired it to be ignored. If Jeannie was still sleeping she wanted her to be wakened. So great was her need to unburden herself of her anguish that if Jeannie was still abed Ruth knew she would be unable to restrain herself from rushing to fling herself down beside her sister-in-law and sob out her wretchedness.

Susan, still clutching Gruntly Finny and little more than half awake, kicked off her sandals and climbed on to the settee. Her thumb went firmly into her mouth as if she was intent on recapturing sleep as quickly as she could.

'I want a drink of water,' said Simon and followed by Heather went through to the kitchen. A second later they were back. 'Mummy! Mummy!' they shrilled.

Ruth almost collided with them in her haste to get to the kitchen. The door was open and entering she was assailed by the smell of stale tobacco smoke. Swiftly her eyes took in the barewood table top now littered with crumbs and stained by slopped tea; the three plates besmeared with congealed fat and egg yolk; the spilled sugar around the empty, upturned basin; the mugs with their dregs of cold tea; the tumbled chairs; the red-tiled floor liberally spattered with cigarette ash and blotched with what looked like half-dried spittle; the white roller towel shamed by dragged and filthy fingermarks. Sickened she turned away and met the incredulous stares of Heather and Simon; she saw fear surge back into their expressions.

'Into the car quickly, children!' she ordered and picking up Susan ran with them to the car. Before her dilemma had time to beat into her stunned brain she had started the engine ready for flight.

'I think some of the bad men must have broken into Aunty Jeannie's kitchen while she was out,' Heather remarked in a small, tremulous voice.

'Yes,' Ruth's acknowledgement was equally tremulous.

'We ought to go and look for Aunty Jeannie,' Simon reminded her.

Shame chafed at her mind. 'Yes, of course we must.' She bit her lip. 'Children,' she managed to say steadily. 'I want you to stay here in the car and look after one another while I go and look to see if Aunty Jeannie is anywhere about.'

'I want to come with you,' Simon declared.

'Me too,' Heather began insistently, thereby triggering off plaintive entreaties from Susan.

The vehemence of Ruth's refusal silenced their rising protests. 'I shall take Tansy and I shall take Simon's stick. I want you to lock yourselves in the car but be ready to open the door for me if I come running quickly out of the house. If you should see any strangers I want you to shout out and make as much noise as you can so I shall be able to hear you. Understand?' They nodded abjectly. 'You'll be all right,' she told them. 'Why not start counting the seconds and then you can tell me exactly how long I've been away from you?' She tried not to be affected by the mute entreaty in their expressions. 'Look after one another,' she reminded Simon.

The fact that earlier, when she had had the run of the house, Tansy had not given any indication of the presence of strangers allayed to some extent Ruth's fears that the marauders might still be on the premises. But perhaps Tansy had not investigated upstairs?

'Hie on, Tansy!' she commanded and immediately Tansy ran ahead and entered the house. Ruth followed cautiously, peering into the kitchen and then the living room, checking they were still as they had left them a few minutes previously. When she was satisfied she signalled Tansy to go upstairs. Tansy complied delightedly and when, after a few seconds of exploration, she came and stood at the top of the stairs, wagging her tail as if inviting someone to join her in play, Ruth gained courage enough to follow.

The doors of the two bedrooms and the bathroom were standing wide open as Jeannie liked them to be in the hot weather and Ruth, noticing nothing so far amiss as well as being reassured by Tansy's total lack of interest, went warily into Jeannie's room. With a great sigh of relief she saw it looking as serene and tidy as always; the bed made and covered by a patchwork

60

quilt. So Jeannie had either not slept in the bed last night or she had gone out early, making the bed before she went, Ruth reasoned. She looked under the bed and in the cupboards and inspected the other rooms similarly without finding any trace of the attentions or presence of any marauders. Evidently they had confined their misbehaviour to the kitchen. But where were they now? And where was Jeannie that she had not returned when they themselves had arrived? The pervasive fear that all was not well with Jeannie deepened the furrows of Ruth's brow, but as she returned to the car she tried by lifting her eyebrows to lighten her expression.

'We can all go back into the house,' she told the children. 'Aunty Jeannie's not in there so she must be out in the fields. I expect she'll be back quite soon.' She spoke with a conviction she was far from feeling. 'Meanwhile we may just as well start taking some of the bits and pieces we've brought into the house.' The children looked unconvinced. 'We won't put them in the kitchen,' she said. 'We'll put them on the living room table for now.'

Once inside the house they began clamouring for food. Ruth knew what they were expecting. One of the delights of their visits to the farm was the abundance of frothy, fresh milk and the well-filled tins of cookie biscuits which Jeannie baked so expertly and offered so lavishly.

'Very well,' said Ruth, spurring herself to sham purposefulness. 'You find our own mugs and dishes and a packet of cereal and then we can all have some breakfast while we're waiting for Aunt Jeannie. I'll go and get some milk from the larder,' she told them, heading in the direction of the larder.

Opening the door she recoiled as if she had suddenly discovered herself standing on the edge of a precipice. Her horrifed eyes travelled to and fro along the bare shelves where the smashed bread crock, the spilled milk-setting bowls and the lidless cake tins flagrantly proclaimed that the customarily well-stocked larder with its shelves of bottled fruits and its store of home-made jams and cakes had been savagely ransacked. Broken glass littered the floor; sticky juice congealed on the shelves; the only traces of the larder's former plenty were a few bunches of dried herbs trodden among the debris on the floor like withered blooms discarded from a grave. The evil presence of the intruders still tainted the dim coolness and as she turned away and slammed the door Ruth was so gripped by anger that she could not stifle the vituperation which rose to her lips.

'There's no milk nor any other food or drink in the larder,' she told the children bitterly. 'Whoever made this mess in the kitchen has made an even worse one in there.'

Simon shot her a look of startled disbelief and went himself to inspect the larder. There was a moment of shocked silence before he too slammed the door. When he returned his face was red and contorted as if he had just received an unexpected slap. 'It doesn't even look like Aunty Jeannie's larder any more,' he exclaimed, throwing himself dejectedly into a chair. The two girls rushed to see for themselves and to gasp at the shambles of what, to them, had always seemed like a secret cave full of tasty surprises which Aunt Jeannie would produce, conjurer-like, whenever they visited her.

'Watch out for the broken glass!' warned Ruth belatedly, and a moment later added, 'And keep Tansy away from it!'

'You'll have to eat cornflakes and sugar, seeing we haven't any milk,' Ruth said when the girls came back.

'I don't want cornflakes without milk,' Susan

grumbled. Simon and Heather also shrugged their distaste.

'It's time Aunty Jeannie was back from milking,' Heather observed. 'These bad men who came and did these wicked things must have come while Aunty Jeannie was out, mustn't they, Mummy?' When Ruth made no reply she went on, 'She's going to be very angry when she sees what's happened, I'm sure.'

'Shall we look and see if she's fed the hens yet?' Simon suggested. 'If she has she will have collected the eggs and then we'll be able to have eggs for breakfast.'

Ruth tried to swallow the dry lump that had risen in her throat. She recalled seeing the poultry waiting at the gate of their pen, anticipating their morning feed. 'I'll just go outside and try calling Aunt Jeannie,' she told the children. 'Her brake's here so she's not likely to be far away.' The children followed her outside adding their shouts to hers but there was no response.

Simon said, 'The hens haven't been fed yet, look, Mummy!' Their eyes met and anxiety flashed between them. 'I know, maybe, what's happened. Maybe the brake wouldn't start and she's gone down to the Biggs's farm to get someone to help her,' he added but she knew he was saying it only to assuage the mounting fears of the other two children.

'Do you think there are any bad men still here?' Heather asked.

'Oh, no!' Ruth refuted the idea with a positiveness she was far from feeling.

'Then I think Aunty Jeannie would like us to feed the hens,' Heather advised. 'Anybody can see they're hungry and it's cruel to make them wait for their breakfast. I'm surprised at Aunty Jeannie because she usually feeds them very early.'

Ruth hesitated, scanning the farm buildings for signs of disturbance before she agreed. 'Yes, I think you're right, Heather. I think that's what we should do.' She led the way to the mealshed, glad that the ever curious Tansy was as usual eager to precede them. She had hardened herself to face further depradations but mercifully the mealshed betrayed no evidence of intruders. A pile of neatly folded meal sacks looked intact and beside them stood an almost full sack of what she recognized as poultry grain with its top rolled carefully open.

'The sack should have its measure sticking out of it,' Heather recalled confidently. 'It's blue and when it's filled to the brim it's exactly the right amount for the hens. It's always kept here except when Aunt Jeannie has it with her.'

'Then she must have it with her now,' said Ruth. 'Perhaps she needed it for something else.'

'Maybe it's buried itself deeper in the sack,' suggested Simon.

Eagerly the children plunged their hands into the wide, full-bellied sack and, momentarily released from the tyranny of fear, they began delving competitively, deeper and deeper, revelling in the feel of the cool, slippery grain on their bare arms and spilling it liberally as they allowed it to trickle through their fingers. Despite her impatience to get back to the house Ruth stood watching them indulgently, neither hurrying them nor chiding them. Jeannie, she was sure, would understand about all the spilled grain.

'It's not here,' Heather at last declared. 'We'll just have to use the calf nut measure and fill it twice.'

They fed the poultry and Heather collected the eggs. 'Only eight,' she remarked derisively. 'Aunty Jeannie usually gets about fifteen in the mornings.'

'It's early yet,' Ruth reminded her.

Before returning to the house they stood together, cupping their hands to their mouths and shouting as loudly as they could for their aunt but there came no response. Ruth's longing for her sister-in law suddenly to hail them grew more frantic. Surely Jeannie would come soon, light-footed and waving a welcome? She wondered if she should take the children down to the Biggs's Farm to find out whether they had seen Jeannie or could give an account of where she might be. Had she perhaps sought refuge there when the attackers had invaded her home? It would have been the most sensible thing for her to have done, Ruth thought.

The clock above the stove choked out the hour of nine. Surely Jeannie should be home by now? Taut with worry she said, 'Children, I think I must go and look in the outbuildings in case Aunt Jeannie has had an accident of some sort. She could have tripped and fallen and may be in need of help. You stay here for just a few moments while I go and look.'

'Aunt Jeannie wouldn't still be in any of the buildings,' Simon stated. 'She'd have heard us shouting and would have shouted back.'

She knew he was right but asked herself what danger she might be exposing them to by allowing them to accompany her? Would they not be safer in the house for the few minutes she expected to be? 'She may not have heard us,' she argued. 'She could have fainted.'

'I don't want you to go by yourself,' Simon said.

'No, Mummy, no!' implored the two girls, rushing to hold her.

'Look, children,' she reasoned. 'I've got to try and find Aunt Jeannie. Simon, I know you'll be sensible and strong and look after everything. I'm only going to do a quick sprint around and I can be much quicker on my own.' Simon looked at her with doubtful acceptance.

'Can we stay here by the door and watch you?' he asked hopefully.

Ruth considered for a moment before nodding agreement. 'But don't attempt to follow me unless I signal that I want you,' she stipulated. 'And if you do see any strangers go inside and bolt the door. Don't open it to anyone but me.'

'Be sure to take Tansy, Mummy,' Heather advised. 'And take Gruntly Finny so if you want Tansy to bite anyone you can just squeeze him, like Susan did in the car.' Without demur Susan yielded up her precious teddy bear.

'I'll certainly do that,' Ruth promised. 'Now remember none of you must move away from the house unless I call you.' Their dread of being left alone was so plain she felt torn by her own decision. She tried to think of something she could say or some small task she could set them that might help to fill the short void of her absence. Her eye lit on Susan's sandals. 'Will you help Susan put on her sandals and make sure she gets them on the right feet. Uncle Guardy got them mixed when he put them on for her.' It was a limp enough expedient but her mind was too cluttered to devise a better one.

When she stepped outside she paused, fighting her own misgivings at leaving them alone. When she glanced back to reassure herself she saw they were standing rigidly together, their eyes holding her as compulsively as reins, and when she sped across the yard towards the buildings she felt as if she was straining against a rubber rope that continually pulled her back towards the house. 'Oh, Lord God! Lead me to Jeannie!' she beseeched, audibly now since there was no one to hear. 'Dear God! Don't let anything have happened to Jeannie!' But she knew even as she prayed; knew with a total heart-sickening certainty that something had happened to her sister-in-law. 'Jeannie!' she called repeatedly as she approached the byre and listened hard for the faintest sound of a reply. The byre was empty and swept clean and she remembered that of course the cows would be out in the meadow at this time of year. She made a perfunctory but sufficient inspection of several other sheds and finding them all empty crossed over to the barn which, again because of the time of year, was empty save for a few bales of the previous year's hay tumbled and strewn at the far end. And then she noticed the scattering of grain on the floor and her eye followed the trail to where the missing blue grain measure lay near the tumbled hay. 'Jeannie!' she called, her voice rasping in her dry throat. 'Jeannie! Are you here?' But her calls were only thrown back at her from the iron roof. Fear was becoming skin-tight and as she stood summoning up her dwindling courage there was a doleful howl from Tansy at the far end of the barn. Fear drained Ruth's strength; she felt as if her whole body were a labyrinth with fear exploring every secret way and urging her to turn and run back as quickly as she could to the children. But she knew she had to investigate whatever it was Tansy had discovered. Taking a firmer hold of the heavy stick she goaded her quaking legs to carry her forward to where Tansy was still standing stiffly, one paw uplifted and her attention riveted on something among the hay bales.

'Jeannie!' Ruth's cry was half moan, half protest as she stumbled forward to crouch beside the figure that lay spreadeagled on the hay. 'Jeannie! Jeannie, love!' She lifted Jeannie's hand and finding it limp and chill put an arm under her shoulders and attempted to lift her. Her arm slid away and Jeannie's shoulders dropped back against the hay. 'Dear God! No! No!' The denial burst from her as if she had been punched hard in the stomach. She pressed her hand against her mouth, stifling the screams that fought to burst from her throat. Slowly she rose to her feet, wilting against the hay bales and closing her eyes to shut out the sight of Jeannie's blue eyes, so beautiful in life, now staring glassily. When she opened her own eyes again she took in the implication of the torn clothes. She could feel her flesh actually creeping and a rising revulsion coalesced with an immense anger; an anger so fierce that it screwed up her stomach until she retched and retched again. The retching was succeeded by a dreadful inertia through which her own breathing seemed to be coming in stertorous gasps. She had the sensation that her body had been so fragmented by the impact of her discovery that it needed time to reassemble itself before it could function. It wasn't true that Jeannie was dead. What her eyes were seeing was being contradicted by her brain. Jeannie, her much-loved sister-in-law; Jeannie, David's only sister; her children's adored aunt. Jeannie was dead! Jeannie had been murdered! Like a malevolent hissing the truth pierced ever more insistently into her comprehension. The hissing swelled and surged and eddied, entangling itself with a dark mist that threatened her vision. She braced herself to combat it. I mustn't faint, she rebuked herself. I must not faint.

A tiny sound prodded her into instant vigilance and dreading it might be the children coming to look for her she found the strength to hasten forward to intercept them. But it was only a bird disturbed by Tansy's explorings and protesting as it flew out into the sunlight. Along with a slight jerk of relief came a pulsing urge to return to the children and she hurried outside, bolting the door behind her with a conveniently high bolt out of the reach of the children should they chance to come this way. She would come back later and cover Jeannie, she promised herself. Weakly she leaned back against the door clenching her fists tightly and drawing deep breaths while she nerved herself to face the questions she knew would come.

Simon was watching for her outside the door of the cottage, obviously worried by her absence. She waved, indicating she was now returning, but though instinct urged her to run her feet still felt too leaden for haste.

How was she going to break it to them that their aunt was dead? Should she prevaricate, saying only that she had been unable to find Jeannie? Might it not be advisable to delay telling them the truth until David was with her to help cope with their reaction? How then would she explain Jeannie's continued absence? How long could she hope to conceal the truth from them? As the questions churned away unanswered there came the realization that whatever she told them would only add to their disquiet.

'You were a long time in the barn, Mummy,' Simon greeted her fretfully.

'Was I?' She went inside and closing the door sat down heavily in a chair. Something about her seemed to gag the children's questioning. They gathered around her, their eyes wide with dumb appeal, fixed on her face.

It was Heather who spoke first.

'Have you found Aunty Jeannie, Mummy?'

She nodded slowly, her eyes blinded by tears.

'She's not dead, is she?' faltered Simon.

Her lips moved soundlessly but her head nodded slow assent. The two girls wailed loudly, their small bodies shaken by sobbing. All three children flung themselves at her, seeking the solace of her outstretched arms.

'What happened to her, Mummy?' Simon controlled his grief sufficiently to ask.

The phrasing of his question gave her a chance to spare them the whole grisly truth. 'I think she must have fallen and hit her head,' she improvised. 'I don't know how it could have happened but she's there in the barn.'

'Are you quite sure she's dead?' Simon pursued.

'Quite sure,' she affirmed. 'I couldn't believe it myself at first.' The children, having paused to listen to her explanation, again gave themselves up to paroxysms of weeping. She ushered them into the living room and sat with them on the settee, and because there were now so many tears Ruth no longer tried to hold back her own. The room became a dreariness of weeping. Gradually the sobbing gave way to moaning; moaning gave way to whimpers; whimpers to broken sighs; sighs to slumber. Looking at them Ruth was overwhelmed by a tearing compassion and an aching yearning to protect them from the hideousness of events. Crushed by the knowledge of her own limitations she flung herself down on her knees beside an armchair and there, cradling her head in her arms, she closed her burning eyelids and implored, with voiceless fervency, that her Maker would give her strength and guidance.

The sudden suspicion that she might have neglected to secure the outer door when she had come in brought her to her feet with a jump and sent her hurrying noiselessly through the hallway to shoot the weather bolts designed to hold the door against the bullying storms. Passing the kitchen her eye lit on the soiled roller towel and in a frenzy of hate and rage she tore it down and hid its foulness in the bin. Peeping in at the children and finding them still asleep she returned to the kitchen admitting to herself the desperate need to be solitary if only for a few minutes so her mind could, without interruption, juggle with the problem of what to do until David and Clyde arrived.

With her lips still moving in prayer she sat in the rocking chair, rocking gently, lulled by its faint rhythmic creakings. The tap over the sink dripped steadily. The wall clock ticked on indifferently.

6

A small sound jerked Ruth into a new alertness. Simon, having wakened and disentangled himself from the arms of the two girls without rousing them, had come through to the kitchen in search of her.

'Shall I make you a cup of coffee, Mummy?' he asked softly.

She made a tired gesture of refusal. Earlier she had been longing for a coffee but now her stomach felt too cramped to cope with either food or drink. Nevertheless Simon filled the kettle and put it on the stove. When it boiled he found instant coffee in one of the bags they had brought with them. Carefully he carried a steaming cup over to the table beside her.

'Try to drink it, Mummy. You always say a cup of coffee makes you feel better,' he coaxed.

She closed her eyes, fighting the nausea that rose within her. 'I'm truly sorry, Simon. But my throat feels so tight I couldn't swallow anything just yet. It would choke me.'

He looked at her commiseratingly with eyes that were still swollen with tears and sitting down beside her he sipped at the coffee, grimacing as he did so. He didn't like coffee without milk but since his Daddy never took milk or sugar in coffee Simon was determined to acquire a taste for it that way. After a few sips he pushed it away. 'Did someone kill Aunt Jeannie?' he asked in a stiff voice.

Ruth looked at him and the depth of despair in her eyes answered his question.

'We ought to tell the police,' he said.

Ruth sat up. She had been intending as soon as the

children wakened to go down to the Biggs's farm for help but of course Simon was right. She must contact the police! Though she had been too distraught to recognize it until this moment she realized that the need to do so had been ticking away at the back of her mind ever since she had discovered Jeannie's body. Now Simon's words triggered the ticking into an explosion and she went quickly into the hallway, pulling the door of the living room gently shut as she passed. Before she had picked up the receiver she knew it was unlikely she would get through but she dialled just the same and was seized with a fleeting hope when she heard faintly, as if at a great distance, the gabble of voices. 'Hello! Police! Emergency!' she shouted but only a few clickings interspersed with the gabblings rewarded her efforts. She continued dialling and shouting her message in the hope that her voice might be audible to some listener who was inaudible to her. 'Police! Murder!' Unwittingly her voice grew louder as her despair and frustration mounted and Simon, who stood in the doorway, signalled to her, putting his fingers to his lips. But it was too late. Her shouting had wakened the children and they burst into the hallway, their eyes dilated with terror.

'Mummy! Mummy! Why are you saying "murder"? Who's been murdered?'

As she put down the receiver Ruth was again swept by a sense of failure. She had wanted to spare them from knowing the brutal truth.

Simon said, 'Aunty Jeannie was murdered by the bad men who were here, wasn't she, Mummy?'

The screaming broke out again but now it was panic not grief which was responsible.

'Will they come back and murder us?' they sobbed. 'Oh, please, Mummy, let's all go back to The Braes and wait for Daddy.'

As she tried to comfort them she felt crushed, as if

she had been physically beaten almost to the point of insensibility and she knew at that moment that had there been anyone else to take charge of the children it would have been easy to surrender herself, body and soul, to a state of total oblivion. But there was no one else. Until her husband and Clyde arrived she must subjugate her own torment and carry on. In the presence of the children she must resist even the indulgence of resting her throbbing head in her arms in case the sight of her doing so should add to their consternation.

Going through to the kitchen she cupped her hands under the cold water tap and sluiced her face. The water was balm to her aching brow, restoring her sufficiently to coerce her thoughts into grappling with their situation.

'Darlings,' she began, turning to the children. 'We can't go back to The Braes so we must all have a little talk about what we must do until Daddy comes. It's not likely the bad men will come back so we'll be safe enough here if we keep the doors and windows locked.' Simon and Heather listened attentively. Susan, claiming her mother's lap, sucked her thumb as she tried to concentrate on what Ruth was saying.

'You've all been very brave,' Ruth continued, 'and you must stay brave and do your best to look after one another until Daddy and Uncle Clyde get here.' The children nodded sombre understanding. 'And we must try not to think about the sad and horrible things that have happened and instead think of things we must do now. It will help us all to do that. We've all been very frightened. I know we're still frightened and we must all keep a good look-out until Daddy and Uncle Clyde come.'

'When Daddy and Uncle Clyde get here I shan't be frightened any more,' Heather said. 'Not like I was in the car.'

'I was the most frightenedest of everybody,' claimed

Susan. 'When that bad man was trying to get into the car I was so frightened I thought my skin was going to shiver right off me.'

The hint of rivalry made Ruth say, 'Shall we talk about what we must do while we're waiting for Daddy? I know I must stoke the stove in case it goes out but what about other jobs? I've got a headache and can't think clearly so will you help me?'

There was a full moment of silence before Heather turned to look directly at Ruth. Against the pallor of her face her widening eyes were like spreading inkspots on white blotting paper. 'Will we have to dig a hole and bury Aunty Jeannie like we did when Freddy, my guinea pig, died?'

The small wounded voice, the total unexpectedness of the question cracked Ruth's flimsy composure. 'No!' She snapped out the denial with unintentional vehemence and then, aware of their startled faces, she said more calmly, 'No, darlings. Don't think about that. Daddy will be here and he'll take care of all that.' She was ashamed of the dismissive tone of her reply. Dear God! came the piercing thought. What stark images a child's mind can conceal! Cutting short the intolerable tension she said quickly, 'Anyone thought of jobs we should do?'

Simon proposed, 'Someone ought to milk Buttercup.'

Ruth considered, recalling that when she had looked in the byre during her search for Jeannie there had been no calf in the calf pen. 'Doesn't Aunty Jeannie bring the calf in at night so it can't suckle Buttercup? Then doesn't she take what milk she wants from Buttercup before she lets the calf suckle?'

'Yes, that's right,' Simon agreed. 'There wouldn't be any milk in the mornings if the calf stayed with Buttercup.'

'The calf wasn't in the byre this morning,' Ruth said.

'It must still be with Buttercup, then,' said Heather.

'In that case there won't be any milk left,' Simon reasoned. 'Or not much,' he added.

Much as she would have liked fresh milk for the children and for herself Ruth was relieved there was no need to go out to the meadow and find Buttercup and milk her.

The sun was shining in through the closed windows and the kitchen, already warmed by the continuous burning stove, was becoming uncomfortably hot. The children were growing lethargic and Ruth, suggesting they should go through to the relative coolness of the living room, found them comics and picture books from among the variety of bags and parcels they had brought with them. She watched them as they settled themselves down and was racked by the apparent anguish which, in just the last few hours, had graven itself on their young faces. The face of any child stricken with apprehension was always enough to arouse Ruth's immediate compassion. Now it was her own children who were the victims. Again there coursed through her a fierce impulse to gather her children in her arms and try, by loving assurance and promises, to dispel their wretchedness. But knowing it would result in a renewed outbreak of grief and that grief had already taken a heavy toll of their spirits and hers, she had to quell the impulse. It eased her mind fractionally to see that they were no longer crying but she was only too aware that when they murmured together their voices were broken with frequent sobs and she suspected their intense concentration on their comics and books was largely a defence against spates of tears.

She said, 'I'm going to take blankets and things upstairs and make up the beds ready for tonight. Just stay where you are until I've finished.'

'I'll come and help,' Simon volunteered, following her through to the kitchen.

Before she began on the blankets Ruth searched in

her handbag for aspirin. She was filling a glass with water when she heard the sound of a vehicle approaching. For an instant she and Simon stared at each other wild-eyed with panic but then with a stab of relief they saw a police van turning into the driveway. When the driver alighted she recognized him as the local policeman and unbolting the door she went out to meet him.

'Thank God you've come!' she greeted him and poured out her story. He listened impassively with only an oblique glance in the direction of the barn.

'I'll go and look,' he said.

Ruth reached out as if to lay a detaining hand on his arm. Her mouth opened but her throat clenched on whatever it was she wanted to say, and she could only point tremulously as she strove to focus her eyes on his face which first loomed close and then receded. Her bones felt as if they were melting and as she swayed she felt the beginnings of a scream welling up in her throat. 'Steady!' The policeman's voice penetrated her dulled hearing and opening her eyes she found she was sitting on the grass verge beside the van with his arm supporting her shoulders. Behind him hovered Simon, shakily proffering a glass of water.

'The other children?' she cried out as full consciousness returned. She tried to rise but the policeman's arm was firm and she sank back. He held the glass of water to her lips.

'They're all right. They're shut in the house,' Simon was quick to assure her.

She managed a feebly grateful glance at him before her eyelids fluttered and closed again. 'I suppose I fainted,' she murmured.

'You did,' said the policeman. 'You should be okay now, though. All the same I shouldn't try to get up until you feel a bit stronger. You'd be best staying where you are until I get back.' She saw him take a rolled up bundle from his van before he set off with his official, purposeful stride towards the barn.

Testing her strength Ruth again attempted to rise. Simon watched her with a worried frown and made no effort to assist her.

'The policeman said you should stay where you are until he gets back,' he reminded her. 'Please do what he says, Mummy.'

'Very well,' she acquiesced, perturbed at her lingering weakness.

Simon looked at her intently. His lip was caught between his teeth and he was valiantly trying to combat tears. 'Mummy, you aren't going to die, are you?' he beseeched with such earnestness that she lifted her arms and drew him close.

'Oh, Simon, no. Of course I'm not going to die. I only fainted.' Her voice was gentle with loving understanding and for a few moments he lay against her breast. Then, sitting up, he wiped the sleeve of his shirt across his eyes. 'I thought you were going to when I saw you nearly fall,' he confessed somewhat shamefacedly.

She tousled his hair tenderly. 'Well, I'm not,' she told him and gave him the nearest approach to a grin she could manage.

Looking up she saw the figure of the policeman approaching. He looked white and grim-faced as he bent to pick up the empty glass.

'Will you go and fill this up again?' he asked, handing Simon the glass. 'I think it would do your Mummy good to stay here for a minute or two longer until she gets her strength back.' When Simon was out of earshot he went on, 'I've seen the body and will make my report. It will be taken care of as soon as things can be arranged. Don't be fretting yourself about details. I've covered her and we'll contact her parents and make the necessary arrangements. You can leave everything to us.'

His term 'the body' for the vital, lovely and loving Jeannie seemed in itself a violation and Ruth's mind blanked off so she missed what he was sa ng until his voice changed, compelling her attention. 'By God! I'd like to get the villains responsible for it,' he burst out, visibly shaken. 'What harm did Jeannie ever do anybody? She hadn't an enemy in the world.' He looked away as if ashamed of his outburst, and distraught as she herself was Ruth could not help noticing the lines of strain on his young face.

'Thank God I managed to contact you!' Ruth said. 'The telephone didn't seem to be working and I doubted very much whether you'd got my message.'

A spasm of surprise crossed his face. 'Message?' he repeated. 'I didn't get any message from you. The telephones aren't working. I reckon the exchange is likely to be out of action for a day or two yet.'

'No message about Jeannie?' Ruth asked in astonishment. 'I thought it must have got through when I saw you arrive.' Her voice trailed off as if she had lost the thread of her supposition. 'But you came, didn't you?' she said pointedly. 'Why?'

'I came to deliver a message,' he began, his voice reverting to its official tone but as swift talons of dread clutched at her Ruth interrupted him.

'My husband?' she whispered. 'Has there been a message from my husband?' Her tight-held breath escaped in a sigh of relief when he shook his head negatively.

'No, the message was for Jeannie but it applies to you now you're here. You and the children must leave at once,' he went on inexorably. 'The military are taking over the whole of this area and we've got to get all civilians out immediately.' He seemed embarrassed by the dumbfounded way she was staring at him and his voice took on a stricter tone. 'It's my job to ensure everyone leaves,' he said, and added more compa-

78

sionately, 'They're not expecting you to go on foot. There's an issue of petrol.' Going to his van he lifted out a can of petrol and placed it beside her own car. 'That's yours,' he said. 'Enough to get you out of what's considered the danger area.' Again his voice hardened. 'But see that you get moving quickly. You must be away from here within the hour at most.'

Ruth was still staring at him uncomprehendingly when Simon returned with the re-filled glass. She gulped eagerly at the cold water, hoping it would help her voice the protestations which rose to her throat. Had she not already reached the limits of her endurance? Surely no one could expect her to embark on yet another hazardous journey when there was only herself to protect three young children? Surely someone in authority would understand that she must wait here until her husband returned? Objections spun round and round in her mind.

'My husband,' she began. 'He and Clyde, the children's uncle, they could arrive here either tomorrow or the day after. They're bringing back *Moonwind*, Dave's fishing boat after her refit. I left word with the coast-guard at the Port that we'd be here and he promised to try his best to get a signal to *Moonwind*. Couldn't we be allowed to stay until they get here?'

The policeman's expression was uncompromising. 'No, madam. No one will be given permission to stay here and I'm certain your husband's boat will be inter-cepted before he reaches here. You must understand things have taken a very serious turn and it's for their own sakes people are being ordered to leave. The military aim to make a wide surround of the area and drive the rebels towards the Port. The military won't be playing games,' he explained with straining patience. 'And delay in getting your children away from here would result in their being exposed to increased danger.

You wouldn't be willing to risk that, would you?' he challenged severely.

Seeing the stunned look on his mother's face Simon interjected, 'You mean we've got to leave here now? This very minute? Without waiting for Daddy?'

'That's it, laddie. And the sooner you get going the safer you're likely to be.'

Ruth struggled to her feet. 'What will happen to my husband? How will he find us?'

For a moment the policeman looked nonplussed. 'If the coastguard managed to contact him your husband will most likely make for the Cove here. There's a good enough mooring there for his boat, would you say?'

'Oh yes,' agreed Ruth. 'We've come to the Cove quite often when the weather's been good.'

'In that case there shouldn't be much trouble getting in touch with him,' replied the policeman. 'I doubt if he'll be allowed to get as far inland as this though.' He looked at her with solicitous enquiry. 'You want me to say anything to him about . . . ?' He inclined his head towards the barn.

Ruth looked at him appealingly. 'As gently as you can,' she whispered. 'Jeannie's his sister.'

The policeman's acknowledgement was perfunctory but understanding. 'I'll tell him you're all safe but he'll want to know where you're likely to be making for, won't he?' he prompted.

'We'll make for his parents' place at the Anchorage,' she supplied.

'You'll be okay there,' he told her. 'You're lucky to have somewhere like that to go. Many haven't. They'll just have to camp out, likely.' He looked at the sky. 'Good job the weather's fine.'

Ruth regarded him wearily. Of course they were lucky to have somewhere else to go but the dread of resuming the intimidating journey was weighing like a heavy yoke on her shoulders.

'I'd advise you to take fresh food and water with you,' the policeman said. 'And if you've a tent it might be wise to take that along too.'

Disconcerted, she said, 'It's not all that far to the Anchorage. We should be there easily by supper time.'

'It's always best to be prepared for the worst at times like this, isn't it?' he reminded her amiably. 'Especially when you've children to be responsible for.' He looked at his watch and became sternly official once more. 'Get yourselves organized and away from here just as quickly as you can, madam,' he instructed. 'I shall be back this way to check in a while.' As he was about to get into his van he called, 'I shouldn't try calling at any of the farms or houses on the way either. You never know who might have been there before you. And remember don't try and get on to the main road. By-roads only until you're over the railway. That's essential. You need to put twenty miles at least between you and this place before you can start thinking you're safe.'

'Are you sure we're going to be safe then?' Ruth called back.

'Who knows? But unless there are unforeseen developments you should be all right. If you take my advice you'll just keep on going as fast as you can until you reach the Anchorage and have your relatives around you.' He pulled the van door shut and zipped out of the driveway.

Ruth and Simon turned to each other, accepting the new crisis with mutual bewilderment.

7

'Mummy,' Simon began hesitantly. 'Don't you think it would be a good idea if we borrowed Aunt Jeannie's brake? It's bigger than our car so we wouldn't be so squashed. It's got knobbly tyres, too, for rough roads.' The expression on his mother's face told him how repugnant the suggestion was to her and he flushed deeply, ashamed of having to sound so tactless yet convinced his suggestion was a sensible one. 'I don't believe she'd mind,' he added with lame insistence.

Ruth was unable to meet his eyes. While every instinct was stirred to rebellion at the idea that they should help themselves to her dead sister-in-law's brake the logic of his idea drilled itself remorselessly into her mind. Even so, a natural aversion aided the seeking of arguments against the suggestion. 'It may sound a good idea on the face of it, Simon,' she allowed, 'but we must remember the brake is bigger and also heavier than our car. It will use more petrol and we haven't got very much.'

'Maybe there's petrol in the tank,' he replied and darted off to look.

While he was absent Ruth had time to think, with a mixture of relief and regret, how responsible he had become in the last few hours. More like a child twice his age.

'The tank's almost full,' he confirmed when he returned. 'With that and the petrol the policeman left us there should be plenty.'

There was tacit agreement in the look they exchanged. 'Let's get going, then,' Ruth said decisively.

Simon's bald announcement to the other children

that they had to leave Aunty Jeannie's home and carry on to the home of their grandparents was tempered by Ruth's more considerate explanation.

'But what about *Moonwind*?' expostulated Heather truculently. 'We can't leave until Daddy comes. We've got to stay here or he won't know where to find us.' Her lips pouted and her eyes grew stormy.

'No, no,' Ruth hastened to placate her. 'The policeman has promised to meet Daddy as soon as *Moonwind* comes into the Cove and he'll tell Daddy what has happened and where to find us. Then Daddy and Uncle Clyde will carry on in *Moonwind* down to the Anchorage and we'll all be together in Granny and Grandpa's house. You know you always love going to visit Gran and Grandpa, don't you?'

Heather accepted her statement dubiously.

'There won't be any more bad men at Granny's, will there?' Susan asked falteringly.

'No,' Ruth elucidated. 'The reason we have to leave here is because our soldiers want to chase all the bad men from round about here to some place near the Port where they can catch them easily. That sounds sensible, doesn't it?'

'Where are all the bad men, then?' Heather demanded to know.

'According to the policeman they must be between here and the Port. That's why we have to leave quickly so the soldiers can start rounding them up. Try to understand,' she pleaded. 'If you were playing a game that's what you'd be likely to do, isn't it?' When the children nodded reluctant affirmation she said briskly, 'Right then. Come along everyone. We'll start by taking everything we unloaded from the car and putting it into Aunty Jeannie's brake. It's bigger than our car and has stronger tyres,' she added. She had dreaded the questions which would follow her telling them they would be taking the brake but to her surprise the children made little comment. After an initial sluggishness had worn off they began to busy themselves about the task of loading the brake.

'Are we going to take Aunt Jeannie's tent with us?' Simon enquired.

Ruth hesitated, fighting the obsessive guilt of helping herself to yet another of Jeannie's possessions. In spite of the policeman's advice it seemed superfluous to take a tent on a short journey such as theirs would be but the notion that a tent might be of use when they finally reached the Anchorage, coupled with the apparent waste of leaving it behind, prompted her decision. 'Yes, I think it might not be such a bad idea,' she allowed. 'Does anyone know where it's kept?'

'I do,' said Simon and led the way upstairs.

When she had stowed the tent in the brake she paused, giving herself time to make a mental list of other things it might be wise to take with them, and while she stood with the sun warm on her back and the trace of hill breeze cooling her brow she realized with a faint sense of shock that her weariness had now been supplanted by an energy so emphatic that it made her limbs tingle; that her feeling of helplessness and confusion had been ousted by a determination to cope with this new emergency. Going back to the house she set the children to searching in cupboards for any secret stores of food the provident Jeannie might have laid by and while they were thus occupied she ran upstairs to Jeannie's bedroom. Picking up the framed photograph of Jeannie's late husband from the bedside table she studied it fondly for a moment before popping it into the carved wooden box which contained all Jeannie's cherished mementoes. Taking the box out to the brake she pushed it under the passenger seat for safe keeping.

When everything they thought they might need was stowed in the brake it was plain that even with the extra space the brake provided they had far too much luggage. Were they being unduly pessimistic in lumbering themselves to the extent of being unnecessarily cramped? She had to shrug away the problem. There was no time to spare for a reassessment of their likely needs.

'Oughtn't we to lock up?' Simon pointed out as they stood together outside the cottage.

'Yes,' she agreed. 'If I can find a key to lock it with.'

'Aunty Jeannie does have a key. She keeps it in the drawer under the pan shelf,' supplied Heather, who had a talent for scenting out such details.

Ruth found the key and, gnawed by qualms that by so doing she was closing the final chapter of Jeannie's life, she inserted it in the lock and turned it with reluctant fingers. Putting the key in her pocket she called Tansy and went to join the children in the brake.

The sun had spread the day with a brilliant golden warmth that under different circumstances she would have been eager to recognize as an invitation to skimp chores and bask in its glory, but now she shivered, as if the chill inside her was such that it occluded warmth, while her preoccupation with the task ahead left her oblivious of the splendour of the day.

While she waited until the children and Tansy had settled themselves in the brake to everyone's satisfaction Ruth took her last look at the smallholding. Shying away from the barn her glance came to rest on the cottage which for her and her family had always been a haven of such abounding welcome and happiness that abandoning it like this seemed an act of betrayal. She had experienced the wrench of having to leave her own home but then the house had been imperilled by explosions, and the need to escape, coupled with her assumption that their absence would be of short duration, had tempered the pain. But here, set sturdily in the unscathed countryside, the cottage appeared to have a supplicating air as if, having lost its gentle owner, it was now loth to be left to the mercies of strangers. Overcome by despair she turned her back on it. Would they ever come here again, when to do so would be to bare themselves to the stab wounds of memory? She wondered what would happen to the poultry and to the animals all of whom Jeannie had regarded as protegées. She supposed Jeannie's parents would take them to their own farm. But here, nothing would ever be the same again.

Thinking of change made her recognize the change in herself. No longer was she the tolerant, easy-going wife and mother of yesterday, the friendly neighbour. No longer was she the woman she had been only a few hours previously. Her current role, imposed upon her by events, was an amalgam of mother protecting her young; of lone wife steeling herself to ruthlessness; of vengeful sister-in-law nursing cold rage in her heart against the murderers; and in addition, at least until they had reached the Anchorage, she was a confused navigator, knowing in what direction the home of her parents-in-law lay but not knowing how circuitous might be the route she would be compelled to take to reach it.

At the thought of the journey ahead the image of the woman with the child whom she had had to leave beside the road returned to pluck traitorously at her memory, and to the repetitive prayers for help and guidance which, though unspoken, were constantly forming in her mind she added an earnest plea that she might be enabled to acquire a degree of emotional immunity which, in helping her to be less affected by the plight of other sufferers, would aid her in her resolve to get her own children to safety.

Almost as if her prayer had been rejected like a bent coin from a slot machine the sight of the poultry enclosed in their wire run suddenly troubled her. The cows and calves had an abundance of grass to feed on but the poultry, shut away from their main source of food, would have little range for foraging. With a word to the children she hurried across to the run and opening the gate propped it back with a spar of wood. Next she propped open the door of the mealshed. Better the hens should gorge themselves than that the meal should be left for possible marauders to destroy, she thought. And as her glance flicked back to the barn she had a feeling that Jeannie would strongly approve of her action.

* * * * *

At his father-in-law's boatyard which, being wholly a family concern, had been only marginally affected by the general strike, David's boat *Moonwind* had completed her refit save for the final pitching of the re-caulked seams of her fifty-foot deck. David and Clyde had planned that they would leave the yard at dawn the following morning so giving themselves the advantage of daylight for navigating the less familiar and more hazardous waters with which they would have to contend during the first stage of their journey. But David was becoming worried by the news brought in by the few privately owned fishing boats still operating. There were strong rumours that in many places the strikers were out of control; that violence was spreading so alarmingly it seemed the government no longer had power to govern. It needed only a short discussion with Clyde before they agreed that they could just as well do the rest of the pitching themselves after their return to the Port, and so it was that, only a few hours before Ruth and her children were wakened by the explosions, *Moonwind* had topped up with fuel and in the gathering darkness had left the boatyard slip and set sail for the Port.

Neither David nor Clyde had seriously envisaged the

Port as being under threat of attack but as they began to pick up the ship-to-ship radio messages they began to exchange glances of mounting consternation. Going down to the engine room David pushed *Moonwind* to her maximum revs. In the wheelhouse the two men listened intently and when they were not listening for radio messages they themselves were calling repetitively and insistently. When for long minutes the radio was silent they stared ahead trying to discern the long stretches of unlit coastline which normally would have been threaded with identifiable lights. Their thoughts were edgy but unspoken. When they did speak to each other it was in terse, dry-throated monosyllables. David could not keep away from the engine room and, in the nagging frustration of not being able to get even more power out of the engine, he roundly cursed the boat which was his pride.

They spelled each other at the wheel but neither man went to his bunk. They brought each other mugs of coffee and hunks of bread and cheese when the chill of the night made them aware of hunger. Dawn lit the horizon. The day brightened and grew warm, and then the setting sun was flinging crimson mantles across sky and sea before dusk, and then night again, enclosed them.

'Calling *Moonwind*! . . . Calling *Moonwind*! . . . Calling *Moonwind*! . . . Guardy calling *Moonwind*. . . . Are you receiving me? . . . Over. . . .'

The faint calling scratched itself into the tension of the wheelhouse. Instantly David responded. '*Moonwind*; *Moonwind*; *Moonwind*. Receiving you. Receiving you faintly. Receiving you faintly. Over. . . .'

Back in the Port the coastguard, true to his promise to Ruth, had been sending out the thrice-repeated calls intermittently, not from the official coastguard station but from a cave below the cliff path. In his hand he held the small VHF radio with which he had been trying all day to make contact with *Moonwind*. Holding it close to his mouth he had kept his voice down as he called and though he used the correct procedure he substituted 'Guardy' for 'Port Coastguard' in the hope his identity would not so easily be revealed to any quisling informer. It was with a surge of relief that he at last heard David's reply.

'Urgent message! Urgent message! Urgent message!' he called, strengthening his voice. 'Trouble here. Advise do not attempt to enter harbour. Danger. Your family okay. They have gone to your sister's place and await you there. Proceed to Cove. Repeat danger. Advise no lights.' Three times the coastguard repeated the message ending with, 'Are you receiving me? Over. . . .'

'*Moonwind* receiving you. Message clear. Will proceed to Cove. Repeat will proceed to Cove. . . .'

'Over and out!' cut in the coastguard abruptly.

David switched off the lights and *Moonwind*, screened by the dark, sailed on.

The coastguard, having heard a footfall on the path above, slipped his radio into his pocket and retreated stealthily to crouch in the deepness of the cave.

8

Ruth turned the brake out of the driveway, retracing her route down the hill until she spotted the entrance to a narrow, tractor-furrowed lane, which she thought she remembered skirted one or two of the larger farms before it joined up with another lane which wound round the far side of the hill. She could have chosen a less impeding way and still kept clear of the main road as the policeman had instructed but at the back of her mind there was the desire to avoid perhaps harrowing encounters with other refugees who might still be making their way along the minor route.

The sun was high; the sky serene and cloudless. The brake was fast becoming like an oven since Ruth, fearing a recurrence of the incident of the morning, had insisted the windows be closed save for the tiniest fraction of an inch. The children grew more restless with every few hundred yards they travelled.

'Mummy, can't we have the windows open, please,' pleaded Simon. 'I'm beginning to feel sick.' He pushed the damp hair back from his perspiring forehead.

Ruth knew she had to yield, but it was with the firm proviso that should they see anyone or should they have to stop for any reason the windows must immediately be closed.

The fresh air rushed in but so also did the dust from the dry furrows, parching their throats and aggravating the smarting of their eyes. The children were soon murmuring plaintively again and Tansy appeared to be panting exaggeratedly.

'Tansy's tongue's hanging out and she's dribbling all over me,' cried Heather.

'I expect she's thirsty,' Ruth diagnosed. 'But I'm afraid she'll have to stay thirsty. I daren't stop just yet.'

'I think I'm dying of thirst,' warned Heather.

Ruth tried to conceal her vexation. 'Look, darlings,' she told them. 'We're all too hot and we're all very thirsty, but until we get on a bit further I mustn't stop. Now please try to stop grumbling at me and just try swallowing your own spittle for a while.'

'I can get over in the back and get one of the bottles of water,' volunteered Simon. He climbed over the back seat into the rear of the brake but after a few minutes of gasping and struggling his rueful voice came from among the piled-up luggage. 'The water bottles are underneath everything. I can't get at them.'

'Oh, no!' Ruth wailed and sighed exasperatedly over her own lack of forethought. If she was stupid enough to have stowed the drinking water where it could not be reached without first unloading the brake, how negligent was she likely to be in other ways? For one depressing moment she doubted her fitness to carry through her resolve. 'I'm certainly not going to stop yet. We'll have to put up with being thirsty for a while longer.'

The countryside they were passing through was alien to her and she glanced at the mileometer. She glanced at it again quickly, wondering if she had misread the mileage when they had first set out from Jeannie's. She drove on for another half mile or so but when the figures did not change she had to face the truth. 'This mileometer doesn't seem to be working,' she said disconsolately. It would have helped her to swear; to have lashed it with a string of oaths such as she had heard fishermen use to curse the fickleness of the sea or their boats. But she was habituated to not swearing in front of the children, and even had that not been so her vocabulary was far too mild to be satisfying. She told herself the failure of the mileometer was a small if tedious adversity to endure.

'I'm hungry,' Susan announced. 'I want a biscuit.'

Ruth said unhopefully, 'I suppose the biscuits are difficult to get at, too, Simon?'

'Yes,' Simon confirmed. 'I know because I remember putting them in myself.'

'You'll have to wait for biscuits,' she told Susan contritely. Susan pouted.

'I think God is sure to punish the bad men,' said Heather who, having been awarded the third prize for scripture at her school, considered herself to be something of an authority on the ways of the Divinity.

Her statement was received with a chorus of approval from the other two who then subsided into silence save for the occasional mumble of discontent when one of them, trying to wriggle into a more comfortable position, managed to prod a foot or an elbow into someone else; or when the bumps and potholes in the lane were too overdeveloped to be suffered without squawked comments.

Ruth's hands, hot and moist with perspiration, were adhering to the steering wheel but so rough was the road she was unable to release them for more than alternate moments of respite. As she continued negotiating the frequent twists and bends her eyes flicked constantly from left to right intent on detecting the first signs of potential danger. Her foot was ready to tread hard down on the accelerator should it be necessary. Her concentration on the road did not waver even though a portion of her mind had detached itself to beat around the problem of drinks for the children. She was not concerned about food. Much as they might grumble, it would do them no harm to go without food until they reached their Granny's but the day was so stiflingly hot and thirst-making she knew they must all drink soon. She tried to remember how many bottles of water they had put in the car. Was it two or three? They were small bottles admittedly – all they had been able to find – but if they drank sparingly there should be enough to last out the journey. Her problem was that she must stop the car before she could get at the water.

'How far d'you reckon we've come?' she enquired of Simon.

'I'd say about thirty miles,' he estimated.

'I'd think more than twenty, anyway,' Ruth said. 'I think perhaps we could stop if we find a suitable place. Even though we've been travelling so slowly we must have covered at least the distance the policeman recommended.'

'Let everybody keep a good look-out for a place to stop,' instructed Heather. 'Because if I don't get a drink soon I'm going to dry up like a dead ant.'

Despite her reckoning that they were clear of the danger area Ruth allowed a greater margin of safety by driving on for about twenty minutes.

Suddenly there was a shout from Simon. 'There's a bridge! We're coming to a bridge!'

Ruth jumped, thinking he had spotted some hazard, but Simon rushed on excitedly. 'If there's a bridge there might be a stream under it. We could get water without unloading the brake.'

Realizing that her eyes had observed the bridge though her mind had not registered its significance Ruth slowed the car. It was a narrow bridge bounded on either side by a low stone parapet and beyond it, to their right, banks of cropped, sun-crisped grass climbed towards a coppice of tall trees. A meandering fringe of ferns and bushes from a source among the trees and disappearing under the bridge appeared to indicate the course of a hidden stream. She stopped the car and followed by the excited Tansy got out and stood assessing its appeal. 'No, wait until I've had a look around first,' she bade the children who were already petitioning for permission to leave the car. Leaving the door open and keeping a careful look-out, Ruth walked the few steps towards the bridge and looking down over the parapet saw a small shallow pool floored by dark pebbles, confined by moss-covered boulders, and fed by a hurrying cascade of water which, as it emerged from a tunnel of ferns, was splashed copiously with sunlight. How strongly it beckoned her! She listened but no other sound rose above the trilling of water and the rejoicing of larks. There was no perceptible sign of danger.

'Go and get water, Tansy!' she directed and as Tansy pranced down to the pool Ruth pondered whether she dared allow the children to take a brief scamper and refresh themselves. They should be safe here, surely, she reasoned. There were no habitations within sight and she judged it unlikely there would be stray rebels lurking in the vicinity. But she still hesitated. The fact that the road ahead was hidden by a bend troubled her. A vehicle could approach fairly close before they might see or hear it. Her jittery nerves kept her wavering over a decision until she saw Heather had defied her and had got out of the car.

'Heather!' she reproved sternly but Heather stood unashamedly with her hand between her legs and shuffling from one foot to the other.

'Mummy, I can't wait,' she inveigled penitently.

Ruth saw her need. 'All right, darlings,' she yielded. 'You can all get out now for a minute or two.' Eagerly they slid from the car and as soon as they had done so she backed on to the grass, positioning the brake ready for a rapid getaway. Opening the rear doors she dragged out the tent and blankets so as to get at the food and water, and before the children had ceased importuning for drinks there was none left in the bottles. She handed the empty bottles to Simon. 'Run

94

quickly down to the pool and fill these,' she told him, pointing towards the bridge. 'We shall probably need more water before we get to Granny's.'

'Oh, please, Mummy, can't we go too?' Heather pleaded. 'I'm so hot. Please, just for a tiny weeny minute,' she coaxed.

Touched by their beseeching expressions, Ruth gave in. She could keep a strict watch and since the pool was no more than thirty yards away she could have them all back in the brake at the first inkling of danger. 'Very well,' she agreed. 'But remember, the instant I call out you must hare back here quicker than greased lightning. Promise?'

They made sombre, emphatic promises and then, shedding their heat-induced languor, they galloped off down to the pool where, scooping up the cool water in their cupped hands, they bathed their perspiring faces. Ruth watched with a kind of taut indulgence as they knelt, trying to catch the thin cascade of water in their mouths, and then began splashing one another, followed by a retributive chasing across and around the pool with Tansy.

Stretching her own cramped body she forced herself to take slow, relaxed breaths in an effort to unwind her over-strung nerves and at the same time to clear the remembered smell of death which had lingered persistently in her nostrils. She too would have liked to go down to the pool and revel in the feel of the cold water on her hands and face but she was afraid to move so far from the brake and her vantage point. After a short time she called to the children and they came obediently, but when she told them they must carry on with their journey they were reluctant to get back in the brake and pleaded for food.

Again, lulled by the apparent tranquillity of the place she yielded and began to sort out the packages of food.

'Be quiet! I can hear something!' Simon announced.

Ruth paused for a split second of listening and the panic which had, ever since the first explosion, lodged in her throat like a remittent infection, throbbed and swelled to a choking wad. 'Quickly back into the car,' she gulped at the children. They were all in, the doors locked and the windows closed tight; Simon had grabbed his stick and Ruth, with the engine switched on, was holding the clutch ready to drive back on the road, when a motor cycle and sidecar came chugging into sight round the bend. She prayed it would carry on without stopping, but as it drew closer the driver braked and Ruth saw the sidecar was packed to over-flowing with a large-breasted coloured woman and two small dark children. The machine came to a halt and the driver lifted his goggles. She saw that he too was coloured.

'You heard if there's been any news since morning, lady?' the man shouted to Ruth.

She lowered the window just enough to call a reply. 'I've heard nothing.'

The man jerked his head in acknowledgement, unstrapped his helmet and took it off. 'You aiming to get across the main road?' he enquired.

'Yes,' Ruth admitted, still having to shout above the roar of his engine.

'Well, you're not going to get much further along this road,' the man told her. 'The railway bridge further along has gone.'

'Gone?' she echoed, her voice raucous with disbelief. 'It can't have gone,' she told him fatuously.

'It's gone all right. Been blown up. That's why we're here. We can't get to the main road along this way.'

In the few seconds it took for the information to sink into Ruth's mind the man switched off his engine and dismounted from his bike. Ruth, too apprehensive to stop the engine of the brake, continued watching him

96

suspiciously, prepared to let the car leap forward if he made a sudden movement towards her.

'It looks as if we're stuck unless we can go back and find a way,' the man said.

'There must be another bridge further on,' she pointed out.

'How far along?' he asked.

'I don't know,' she admitted. 'I don't know this part of the island very well.'

'Me neither,' the man confessed ruefully. He scratched his head. 'I ain't lived here that long.'

'I know it's no use trying to get back that way,' she nodded in the direction they had come. 'We were ordered out by the police. The military were supposed to be taking over quite a large area. We were ordered off the main road by soldiers,' she added.

'God Almighty!' he exclaimed, still rubbing at his wiry black hair. 'You from the Port, like us?' he questioned. When Ruth nodded confirmation, he went on, 'We've been lucky. God Almighty! It was wicked, I tell you.' His voice became hoarse and he looked down into his upturned crash helmet as if he was about to weep into it. 'We got out pretty quick on the bike but I can tell you it was tough getting through all those people. Some yobbos tried to take the bike from us. They nearly had it but Tossie hit out with a bottle of lemonade she had in the sidecar. Crowned a couple of them, she did, and that's how we managed to get away from them.' He looked affectionately at his wife. 'I never thought I'd see the day when Tossie would lift a hand to a soul, but she did today and likely they'll still be feeling the effects of it,' he finished with malicious satisfaction.

Tossie, who had been staring straight ahead as if she wanted no part in the conversation, now turned to Ruth. 'You protect your own when you have to,' she defended herself.

'We were attacked too,' Ruth responded. 'We only

97

just managed to avoid having the car stolen from us.' She shuddered. 'It was pretty horrible.'

Tossie nodded complete understanding and her husband said, 'I can believe that. You couldn't trust anybody. You had to forget pity and just carry on going. We had to learn that pretty fast, didn't we, Tossie?'

While she listened Ruth was thinking, I too have had to learn fast. Too fast for me to trust you not to try taking over this brake if I give you half a chance. You could easily turn out to be a 'smoothie'.

'Where are you making for?' she asked.

'Tossie's folks, up Craigie way,' the man told her. 'Leastways that's where we set out for but that bridge has kind of messed things up a bit for us.' Again he rubbed at his head as if it helped clear his thoughts. 'Likely we'll get there somewise, some time if the petrol doesn't run out first.' He lifted his shoulders in a resigned way. 'There was enough when we set out but we've been doing so much turning on our tracks since we left the road we might have problems.'

'I'm making for the Anchorage,' Ruth told him. 'The children's granny. I shall simply have to keep on driving until I find another bridge. I have to cross the main road somewhere.'

The man stood with his back to the brake, surveying the main road. He turned to Tossie. 'It looks like there might be water down there,' he said gesturing towards the bridge.

'There is,' Ruth told him. 'A pool of fresh water. The children have just been down there freshening themselves up.'

'Hand me the kettle,' he said to Tossie.

'Tommony Marriott, why would you be wanting a kettle,' began Tossie argumentatively. 'We got no coffee nor tea nor nothing, remember.'

'I can fill the kettle with water, can't I? And then I

can fill the cups from the kettle,' Tommony reasoned. 'You don't want I should go down there and fill four separate cups, do you?' he taxed her.

He lifted the two children from the sidecar and, somewhat stiffly, Tossie heaved herself out. Leaning over the sidecar she eventually extricated a kettle and handed it to her husband. As Ruth watched the family wander down to the pool she was tempted to relinquish a shard of her mistrust. These people appeared to be in much the same plight as she was herself. How good it would be if they could help each other! Her hand strayed experimentally towards the ignition key. Dare she? As if in defiance of her own instincts she reached forward and switched off the engine.

Immediately the children pressed to be allowed out of the brake but she answered their pleas with a fiercely whispered reminder. 'Not yet! We still don't know if we can trust them not to take the brake.'

While she debated whether or not to linger a while longer a bumble bee narrowly missed becoming entangled in her hair as it buzzed in through the open window. Tansy tried to snap at it and the children cowered away. 'Tansy, lie down!' commanded Ruth. 'Don't be frightened,' she told the children. 'If you don't hurt it, it won't hurt you. Just keep quite still.' While she followed its flight, ready to persuade it towards the open window when it should fly near enough, she was aware of a strange feeling of tenderness towards the insect. Its blundering in upon them was such a natural happening – the first sane, uncomplicated happening of the day – and though its presence brought the fear of being stung it was such a small fear, so different from the terror they had endured that it seemed inconsequential. She had assured the children the bee would not attack unless provoked. Now, the thought snarled into her mind that it needed no such provocation for humans to unleash their venom. The bee, finding its way out, zoomed away and as her eyes followed it Ruth found she was curiously grateful for its brief intrusion.

Tossie and Tommony returned with their children. Tommony was carrying the full kettle of water.

'Now we could have a cup of coffee or tea if we had some coffee or tea,' he remarked flippantly.

'We have both tea and coffee,' Ruth was quick to tell him. 'But you aren't going to light a fire, are you? It might attract attention.'

'We wouldn't need to light no fire,' Tossie interpolated. 'We got a little stove.'

'You're well equipped,' Ruth observed.

'We got a pan too but we ain't got nothin' to cook in it.' Tommony managed an ironic chuckle. 'We brought coffee and tea and food with us for Tossie's folks, but they were packed in a case on the pillion and they somehow disappeared when we had the trouble with the yobbos,' he explained.

'We have some food,' Ruth said. 'Not much but you can share what we have.'

'Aw, that's awful kind.' Tossie's coffee-brown eyes glowed her thanks. 'Me an' Tommony we won't take nothin' for ourselves but I wouldn't mind for the kids. They've had nothin' since last night and they've been yammering for it. They don't understand what's happened properly,' she excused them.

'Shall I get coffee?' Simon's hand was on the door handle. 'No,' she whispered. 'Don't get out of the car. Just climb over into the back. It's easy enough to reach now.' Her eyes flashed him a warning. Undesigning as Tossie and her husband appeared to be, had not Tommony himself said there could be no trusting anyone? Not yet, instinct continued to urge Ruth. She must have more proof before she could allow herself to accept the innocence of their intentions.

Simon scrambled back with a half-full jar of coffee

and a packet of tea which Ruth handed through the window to Tossie. 'You're welcome to these,' she said.

'You sure?' Tossie seemed at first reluctant to take them.

'Yes, quite sure. We're not likely to need them. Anyway we've more in the bags.' She indicated Tossie's two children. 'We have some cornflakes too but we have no milk. Will your children eat them dry?'

'They would if they had some sugar to put on them,' Tossie replied morosely. 'Lena and Paul never take milk on cornflakes but they won't eat them without plenty of sugar.'

'We have sugar,' Ruth told her and hardly were the words out of her mouth before Simon was handing her sugar and cornflakes.

'Mummy,' he said in a low voice while Tossie was busy finding bowls for the cornflakes, 'Couldn't we cook our eggs on their stove and eat them now? She said they've got a pan so we could have them boiled or scrambled.'

'No, Simon,' she hissed. 'We mustn't get out of the car.'

'I'm hungry,' he muttered, sliding sulkily back on his seat.

'Kettle's boiling!' called Tommony. 'Lady, you got mugs?'

His question caught Ruth offguard. She had been willing to share what food they had brought with them but she had not envisaged staying to drink coffee with them. Prudence insisted she would be better off on her own and free from the suspicion that Tommony's artlessness was a cloak assumed only until the opportunity to take the brake for himself and his family presented itself. But there was no denying how desperately she wanted to trust them. How much she needed communication with adults; how much she yearned to share a brief suspension from the unremitting stress.

101

'Do you think it's safe for us to stay here?' she temporized.

Tommony shrugged. 'Where's safe?' he countered. 'But there's three of us as well as that big boy you have there,' he nodded at Simon. 'I reckon together we ought to be able to take care of ourselves.' He filled two mugs, one for himself and one for Tossie, and then he waved the steaming kettle invitingly. 'You got mugs, lady?' he asked again. The kindliness of his expression swayed Ruth away from her mistrust.

'I'm no lady, I'm Ruth,' she replied, getting out of the car. 'And yes, we have mugs. I'll get them.' She told the children they could get out of the car, whispering to Simon to stay on guard while she found the mugs in the boot.

Released once again from the car the two girls raced after Tansy back to the pool, but then halted, confronting Tossie's two children who by this time were intent on their bowls of cornflakes.

'Their names are Lena and Paul,' Tommony said. 'I'm telling you that because they're much too shy to tell you themselves.'

'I know without you telling me,' Susan returned condescendingly. 'I was listening when your Mummy told my Mummy.' Tommony looked suitably impressed. 'My name is Susan and I washed my face in the pool down there and I let the sun dry it.' Susan appraised the others by way of introduction. 'And my bear is called Gruntly Finny and our dog is called Tansy,' she continued.

The children regarded one another steadily until, as if by an agreed signal, Lena and Paul simultaneously tipped up their bowls and expertly sucked the remaining cornflakes into their mouths. The next moment all four of them were scampering lightheartedly down to the pool.

Ruth returned to the task of trying to sort out the

food. To her dismay she found that several of the eggs they had brought were cracked to the extent of leaking white and that the butter was in a state more suitable for pouring than spreading. She thought of Simon's request for scrambled eggs.

'I have butter and eggs here,' she called over to Tossie. 'The butter's an oily mess and some of the eggs are broken but did I hear you say you had a pan?' Tossie came over, her mouth opening as the significance of Ruth's invitation dawned on her. 'We could scramble the eggs, perhaps?' Ruth suggested. 'My children have been complaining they're hungry.'

'That's great!' said Tossie, bringing a pan and holding it while Ruth tipped in the butter and eggs. 'It won't take more than a minute to cook up this lot and there'll be enough to keep the children from moaning for food for a while.'

When the food was ready they called the children and Ruth watched while Tossie, with scrupulous fairness, spooned scrambled egg into each proffered bowl. They squatted on the grass while they ate and Ruth dropped to her knees beside them. Thinking her own nerves needed the stimulus of coffee she sipped at the mug Tommony had made for her, but so fierce was the stranglehold of pain and grief the desire to retch threatened as soon as the liquid reached her stomach.

'Yummy! This is like a picnic,' declared Susan artlessly.

'Sure it's a picnic,' Tommony agreed. 'And aren't we lucky to have found a nice place like this to have it?'

The lightness of his tone at first grated on Ruth and she had quickly to remind herself that not only was he trying to jolly the minds of the children but that he and Tossie did not know the full extent of her own tragic experiences. The escape from the Port; the affecting sight of other refugees; the encounters with thugs; these were experiences they had in common. But they had not had to endure the lacerating agony of discovering the body of a beloved relative. They had not found a ransacked and defiled cottage where they had been expecting to find a welcome home. And throughout their ordeal they had had each other's support and strength, while she herself had not only coped alone with three children but had suffered and was still suffering the added strain of not knowing when she would be reunited with her husband.

When the children had scraped the last traces of food from their bowls they drifted back to the pool to resume their play. Tommony, looking speculatively towards the coppice, said, 'I reckon when I've finished this mug of coffee it will be a good idea for me to go and try getting myself a good stick from those trees up there. There might come a need for it yet.' Ruth felt a quick thrust of disquiet. Tommony was big and strong and with him to protect them they would be less vulnerable in case of attack by any stray marauders. But a stick could be an offensive as well as a defensive weapon. 'I reckon I'd best get one for you at the same time, Ruthie,' he suggested.

'Please,' she agreed and was glad none of the children were near enough to pipe up that there was already a good strong stick in the brake. As he sat drinking his coffee she studied him covertly. He sounded so genuine in his concern for her and the children that she had a positive craving to trust him completely. God knows! her spirit cried, how desperately I want to trust them both; to free myself from this torment of suspicion.

'What we going to do then?' Tossie asked.

Gulping down the last mouthful of coffee, Tommony said, 'I reckon we'll have to try and make our way cross country as best we can,' he told her. 'There's bound to be another bridge, as Ruthie says.'

'If they haven't blown that up too,' Tossie reminded him.

'Could be. Could be,' he allowed.

He sounded unperturbed and Ruth assessed him as a man not practised in meeting trouble half way. He got up and began to move away. Ruth rose too, ready in case he should suddenly make a dash for the brake. She pressed a furtive hand on the pocket of her jeans and felt the comforting hardness of the ignition key.

'Don't you go too far away, now, Tommony.' Tossie's tone was anxious.

'God Almighty, Tossie! You don't want that everybody should see what I'm going to do, do you, girl?' he responded banteringly. 'Anywise, did I not say I was going to get us some sticks?' He turned and called to Simon. 'How about you coming along with me to get some sticks, Simon?'

Approaching, Simon glanced at his mother and seeing the sudden doubt in her expression he gave her an almost imperceptible nod of comprehension before calling Tansy to heel and following Tommony. Ruth watched them disappear among the trees managing to hide her nervousness from Tossie by murmuring responses to her conversation while all the time her ears were keyed to pick up every sound from the coppice.

When they emerged from the trees Tommony was carrying two branches that looked as stout as crutches while Simon dragged behind him a stick that looked only slightly less sturdy. Again, as Tommony approached, mistrust stirred in Ruth and like an animal rising at the first scent of danger, she got to her feet, every sinew in her body braced for action.

'Here you are, Ruthie,' Tommony said, holding out one of the sticks towards her. 'That one's for you if you can manage it.' He grinned wryly. 'Keep it by you until you're safely at the end of your journey and then maybe when you get back home you can plant it and

105

watch if it grows.' He became serious. 'I reckon with that and the one Simon has you ought to be able to take pretty good care of yourselves.'

As she put out a shaky hand to take the stick from him she found she could not meet his eyes so ashamed was she of her wavering trust. Now she doubted him no longer. Almost knocked out by relief her knees sagged and she flopped to the ground. Tossie, misunderstanding, said with concern, 'Tommony's not meaning you'll have to use it, love. It's only in case you need it.'

Ruth lifted swimming eyes, unable to explain the reason for her sudden collapse, and while Tommony and Tossie looked on with baffled commiseration her head went down into her hands, her shoulders hunched and she began weeping unrestrainedly. Tossie's eyes glistened and when she put a sympathetic arm around Ruth's shoulders, Ruth clung to her, letting her head rest against the generous bosom. Tossie's arm tightened and she clucked encouragingly, her lips against Ruth's soft fair hair.

Gathering up the dishes Tommony took them down to the pool, muttering that they needed a wash. Simon, who was biting his lips so as not to cry, stood regarding the scene with a kind of truculent misery and seeming to gain some solace by hitting at the hard baked ground with his stick.

Later, when she had recovered herself, Ruth asked Tommony what he recommended should be their next move.

'Pack ourselves up again and carry on,' he replied. 'And the sooner the better,' he added. 'Unless you've got cat's eyes, Ruthie, and can see in the dark.'

She looked up at the sky which was still full of the mellowing afternoon sunshine. There were hours of daylight yet, she reasoned. Even allowing for yet more diversions they surely would have reached their destination before dark. Picking up the stick Tommony had provided for her she called the children and Tansy and hurried them into the brake.

9

While Tossie and her children were inserting themselves into the sidecar Tommony came over to speak to Ruth.

'There's a kind of track you can see from up there in the trees. Not much of a one but it looks as if it could lead some place.'

'Possibly the remains of an old drove road,' Ruth suggested. 'You know, the ones country people used when they walked their stock to market.'

He nodded. 'I reckon if we follow that we'd be sure to come to a bridge or a ford sooner or later.'

An anxious frown creased Ruth's brow. 'D'you think I'll manage the brake along it?'

'I dunno,' Tommony admitted. 'Maybe if we go first on the bike and you follow us. Then if either of us gets stuck the one can help the other.'

'Where do we join it?' she asked.

'Over the bridge here and round the bend first and then we leave the road. That's what looked the best way to me.' He climbed on his bike and kicked the engine into life. Ruth followed just a few yards behind him. Much of the route she had driven along earlier had made progress unnecessarily slow, but after they had left the road and joined the track, such as it was, it proved at times to be well nigh impossible. When it was good it was bumpy as a carelessly ploughed field and tussocked with stiff, waist-high bracken which, the moment it was disturbed, released swarms of blue-bottles to harass them. When it was bad it was formidably so, thwarting their progress with tumbled boulders from the ruined dykes, weed-camouflaged rabbit holes and spiky bracken. More than once Tommony had to call Ruth to go on ahead in the brake because the thickets of brambles were too daunting for him to tackle on the bike. As she revved the engine to forge a way through, the hostile branches clawed at the brake with thorny persistence and, troubled by guilt that it was Jeannie's car which was being so maltreated, she had to deflect her mind from forming senseless apologies that Jeannie would never hear.

The children's murmurings of discontent increased and eventually Susan was driven to cry out fretfully, 'I hate this. It's a horrible place!'

'You'll just have to put up with it,' Ruth retorted. 'There's no other way of getting to Granny's.' A moment later she was penitent. They had endured so much and had been so good through it all. 'Darlings,' she explained. 'Mummy and Tommony are doing our best to get us all out of danger and it doesn't help to have you grumbling and complaining. I'm not enjoying it but I still have to carry on for all our sakes, don't I?'

'I'm not complaining,' denied Simon, and added, 'It's the two girls who are doing all the complaining.'

'I'm grumbling because I feel sick,' Susan defended herself.

'It's Susan's grumbling that's making me feel sick,' Heather excused herself. 'If she'll shut up, I will.'

A sulky silence descended until after little more than half a mile on Tommony signalled he was about to stop. Ruth saw him leave the bike and go forward gingerly testing the ground as he went.

'I think he must have come to a bog,' Simon conjectured. Tommony turned back, making a gesture of acute despair and pointing to his boots which were covered with mire.

'No good!' he called as he approached the brake. 'It stretches thataway and it gets deeper as it goes. I wouldn't be able to haul the bike across let alone you trying it with the brake. We'll need to go back the way we came and see if we can find a way around and about it somewise.'

Ruth managed, after a struggle, to turn the brake but they had proceeded only a matter of yards along the track before Simon called her attention to the fact that Tommony was not following. She stopped and looking back saw Tossie and the children getting out of the sidecar.

'I think he must be stuck in the bog,' Simon said. 'Yes. Look! You can see his wheel spinning and throwing up the mud.'

Ruth got out of the car and went to offer help but with a jerk or two and some skilful manipulation of the handlebars Tommony soon had the bike freed from the bog.

'Mummy,' suggested Simon. 'Wouldn't it be a good idea if Tossie and her children came with you in the brake and then I could go in the sidecar with Tommony? That way I'd be ready to help if we got stuck. And,' he went on, sensing her reluctance to consent, 'I'd be a better look-out than Tossie. She's too busy watching her children don't fall out.'

Ruth was disposed to argue but she knew Simon longed to ride in the sidecar and she had to admit his suggestion sounded a sensible one. 'Simon wants to come with you in the sidecar,' she called to Tommony and left the decision to him.

'We could try it,' he agreed. 'Tossie's likely got a sore behind by now. She'll be glad of a change. Anywise,' he admitted wryly, 'the kids are getting a bit squirmy and she's finding them rather a handful.'

'Oh, my, but this is a comfort after the sidecar,' sighed Tossie thankfully as she sank into the passenger seat beside Ruth while the two children installed themselves with the others in the back of the brake. Ruth smiled vaguely, too hot and too intent on her driving to spare more than a preoccupied nod. Back she drove. Back over the bumps and hollows. Back through the relentless gorse and brambles. Back through the swarms of flies. They were in sight of the coppice above the bridge before Tommony again signalled her to stop.

'I reckon it might be a good idea if you stay here while I go prospecting,' he suggested. 'This is getting us nowhere and taking time and petrol to do it. I reckon I could have walked the distance we've covered and have been quicker about it.' He cocked an appraising eye at a dark glowering cloud just nudging the dip in the hill. 'There's rain threatening too,' he observed. 'That'll mean it might get dark earlier and we can't risk using headlights to see our way.' His smooth brow furrowed in a frown.

Ruth was inclined to agree with him but Tossie was aghast at his proposal.

'Tommony Marriot, you're not going to be allowed to leave us for one minute,' she told him. 'You're staying right here along with us.' As Tommony's mouth opened to argue, Tossie, silencing him with an emphatically raised hand, went on, 'Where you go, we go. You are not leaving us on our own, no, not for one minute,' she repeated vehemently.

Tommony, hunching away mockingly from her raised hand, gave in. 'Okay. Okay. If you say so. You're the boss.' His tone was flippant but the lines on his forehead deepened. With a nod of resignation he went back to his bike and remounted.

When they set off again they climbed above the old drovers' track expecting to find firmer ground, but after about half an hour of what seemed slightly more promising progress the terrain grew even more disheartening than they had previously experienced. Though the bracken was less dense and the gorse and brambles less plenteous the scattered boulders were larger and more deeply embedded; the steepness of the slopes they had to negotiate was so daunting Ruth dared not even ask herself if all four wheels of the brake were on the ground at the same time. Just as frequently as before they had to get everyone out of the brake while a wheel was heaved out of a boghole deceptively camouflaged as a firm-set depression. Everyone grew increasingly sweaty, irritable and finally despondent. Even Tansy who, spurning the slow progress, had deserted the brake to devote herself to flushing out rabbits and chasing them through the undergrowth, trotted now, with lolling tongue and opportunistic glances at the open windows of the brake.

As the sun's heat cooled the swarms of bluebottles retreated to give way to swarms of avaricious midges which fastened on every area of exposed skin. Tossie and her children appeared to be curiously unaffected by the midges – as if their colour acted like a coat of repellent varnish – but Ruth and her children were plagued almost to death by the pestiferous insects. But they had to endure.

They came in sight of a stream beyond which there was a close-packed barrier of trees save where the barrier was divided by a ride which looked wide enough to accommodate their vehicles. However when they had forded the stream and juddered along the ride for some distance they were confronted again by the same stream, but now it had widened into a river which looped around the wood and merged with lesser streams to course downhill towards the valley.

'I reckon our best plan is to find ourselves some good thick cover and make ourselves as comfortable as we can for the night,' Tommony proposed. 'Weatherwise it's still fine enough to sleep out.'

'Sleep out for the night?' Ruth's voice was sharp with argument.

'Lord save us!' exclaimed Tossie with alarm. 'It's not safe!'

'It's safer than trying to find our way in the dark,' Tommony replied. 'Anywise we haven't been molested or seen anything to worry us for the whole time we've been on our way here, so if we're well hidden it's not so likely we'll be disturbed. Maybe a lone rebel or two but we should be a match for them and I'll be keeping watch.' Ruth, knowing he was right, nodded at Tossie. 'There's a good patch of bracken not so far back among the trees – a sort of clearing it was. I reckon it would make a good place,' Tommony finished.

Dispiritedly they retraced their way until Tommony indicated a stretch of bracken that seemed thick and high as a wall. Skirting it he turned the bike and was instantly hidden from view. Ruth followed and found they were in a small clearing hemmed by bracken and reinforced by trees.

Stiff and sore they alighted from their vehicles and assessed their haven for the night.

'This bracken will make nice springy beds for you to lie on while you watch the stars come out,' Tommony inveigled the hesitant children. 'You'll be able to count them popping out. One, two, three.'

'I don't want to watch the stars,' said Susan. 'I want to sleep in the tent.' She clung to Ruth's hand. 'The bad men might come and get us if we sleep outside.'

Tommony looked at Ruth. 'You got a tent?' he asked and, when she nodded, he enquired, 'You want me to help you get it out?'

Ruth stared at him openmouthed. When the policeman had suggested she should pack the tent she had looked at him aghast, and though she had taken his advice she had designated the tent and blankets simply as luggage which might come in useful when they reached the end of their journey. The possibility

113

of having to use it en route had not even edged into the complexity of her thoughts.

She and Tossie helped Tommony erect the tent and spread the blankets. The children, their bodies now limp with tiredness, packed themselves into it with only the odd murmur of discontent when they accused Tansy of helping herself to more than her fair share of the bedding. Within minutes they were sleeping soundly. A misty twilight smothered the sky and the night settled into an enclosed silence through which the churring of a nightjar echoed eerily.

'If you two girls want to get some sleep I'll keep guard,' Tommony offered. 'I was doing a spell of night-work anywise, so I'm conditioned to not sleeping.'

'I don't feel sleepy,' Ruth said and was surprised by the truth of her denial. Though she was conscious that her headache had returned and that to blink made her eyelids feel as if they were lined with abrasive, the goading agony of getting her children to safety seemed to have fortified her body against any cognition of tiredness. Sleep – even the desire for sleep – was unattainable: tiredness was an indulgence which must not be allowed to assail her until they had reached the end of the journey.

'I'm not wanting to sleep either,' Tossie declared and immediately contradicted her statement by stifling a yawn. 'Maybe I'm too scared,' she went on. 'Fright and an empty belly aren't much good as nightcaps.'

'There are some biscuits left but I think we should keep those for the children's breakfast,' Ruth said. 'But we still have plenty of coffee if Tommony thinks it's all right to light the stove.'

'I reckon so,' Tommony replied. 'We're well enough screened here.' He struck a match and the small gas flame spurted into the silence, friendly as a purring kitten.

Walled in by bracken, Tommony, Tossie and Ruth

squatted around the small stove, staring at the confined glow of the flame as if it was a tiny beacon of hope in the darkness, and for the few minutes it took the kettle to boil they experienced a subliminal lightening of their oppression. Once the coffee was brewed the three of them sat together, their backs to the tent flap, sipping slowly so as to make their drink last the longer and talking sporadically in carefully hushed voices. The night cooled and deepened. The mist dispersed to unscreen a scattering of stars which in turn retreated as the moon rose to lean over the shoulder of the hill like a curious neighbour leaning over a fence. Tommony was about to say something when staccato muffled thuds penetrated the silence.

'That sounds just like one of those electric road drills,' commented Tossie with a note of surprise.

'That's gunfire!' Tommony's laconic identification of the noise made Ruth stiffen with apprehension.

'Gunfire?' echoed Tossie, rising agitatedly to her feet.

'Sit down!' Tommony admonished her. 'It's a long way away from here.'

Tossie turned on him indignantly, her hands on her hips. 'You take things too easy, Tommony Marriot,' she accused. 'I'm not waiting here until they come to shoot me.'

'Hush, will you.' Tommony pulled her down beside him. 'Look, Tossie,' he explained patiently. 'It was gunfire all right but it was a long way from here. The sound would carry on a still night like this. Anywise, it's no good you worrying because we can't do anything else but stay here where we're well hidden. We can't leave until it's daylight and by then surely the army will have sorted out the trouble anywise.'

'Or the rebels might have sorted out the army,' Ruth countered.

'Or the rebels might have sorted out the army,' Tommony allowed. 'In that case they'll have got what they wanted so maybe they'll be content to leave plain folks like you's and me's alone.'

'When will it all end and how?' moaned Tossie. She was forgetting to keep her voice down and Tommony shushed her repeatedly. 'How many of us are going to be left alive?' she ended with a stifled sob.

'You be thankful you got your own, Tossie,' Tommony reminded her gently. 'We're all safe here together so you just quit moaning, gel, and say a prayer of thanks for that. You know from what you've seen today we're a lot luckier than some.'

Ruth, staring dry-eyed into the darkness, knew the moment had come for her to tell them about Jeannie. She drew a deep shuddering breath. 'My sister-in-law,' she began. She spoke haltingly in a dry, flat voice, as if the words were being wrung out of her, and while Tommony and Tossie listened their horror and concern was manifested by a stricken silence which lasted until Tossie sobbed out, 'Dear, good Lord! Dear, dear good Lord! You been crucified.'

'Hush, gel. Hush or you'll wake the kids,' Tommony reminded her.

Ruth continued, 'I felt then as if my whole body had disintegrated to the extent I could never be made whole again and I was terrified of not being able to look after the children even until David arrived. Then when the policeman told me we were still in danger and I had to get the children to safety the strength came from somewhere. Some power outside myself seemed to be fitting me together again and sewing me up. That's just how I've felt ever since. Not like myself at all but just a body sewn together with steel wire. I just pray the repair will last until the children and I are reunited with their Daddy.'

The quiet condolence was disturbed by a flying beetle, night-coloured and invisible, which whirred above their heads. Tommony roused himself to brew more coffee.

While they drank they talked bitterly of the calamity that had driven them from their homes. They groped blindly for motives. They reminded themselves of portents which had been glossed over or shrugged aside by the powers-that-be. Gloomily they tried to figure out their own futures.

'What sort of a future is there for us now we've lost our nice little home?' lamented Tossie.

'You don't know that for certain,' her husband corrected her. 'There's a chance it's escaped. You just try looking on the bright side, gel.' Tossie sniffed. 'You just think,' he went on, 'all this could have happened to us in the dead of winter. We might have been stuck out here tonight, us and the kids, in freezing cold and snow. You'd have more to be griping about then, wouldn't you?'

Tossie shivered a protest and Ruth's imagination leaped to see herself struggling through wintry conditions with the children. She resolved not to let the heat worry her for the rest of the journey. 'Yes, you're right,' she admitted to Tommony. 'We could be a lot worse off.'

Tommony said, 'Folks were a lot worse off in the last war than we are now.'

'You don't remember the war, surely?' Ruth asked him. She had grouped him as about the same age as herself.

'Oh, I remember it all right.' His voice was cynical. 'I was only a kid at the time but I have my memories. I lived in London then.'

'Were you bombed out?' Ruth prompted.

'No, our house wasn't hit but the next street copped it one night and then a couple of nights later a big warehouse nearby went up. It was grim, I can tell you. Two of my little cousins I never saw again. My folks had me evacuated to the country then, along with thousands of other kids. Gee, I was scared of the bombs but I think I was just as scared of leaving home without Mammy and Pappy. I reckon I was too scared even to cry. They put us on a train and when we got to this place they loaded all the kids on to buses and took us to a big hall where some women gave us sandwiches and tea and lemonade. Then they made us all sit still and wait while the people came along to choose and collect the evacuees they were willing to take into their homes.'

'It must have been a horrible experience,' Ruth interposed.

'It wasn't so good,' agreed Tommony. 'Of course the prettier and better-dressed children soon got themselves chosen; then the scruffier and cheekier ones. Well, I knew I wasn't pretty but I wasn't cheeky and I wasn't badly dressed. But nobody wanted me. I tried to smile at the folks who came thinking maybe that would help, but white folks were a lot more suspicious then of people with black skins, even kids as young as I was. There seemed to be a good deal of discussion about me among the women; I could tell that by the way they'd whisper together and then turn and look at me as if they wished I'd just disappear. Except for one or two of the other kids nobody spoke to me except to ask me my name, and I just had to sit there waiting and waiting while the place got emptier and emptier as the other kids were taken away. I had a toy monkey I was very fond of and I had to hold on to it for dear life to stop me from crying. It was one of those toys that squeaked when you pressed it and every time I heard a woman say, "No, I'm not taking a nigger into my home", I'd have to make the monkey squeak over and over again to cheer me up. In the end the hall was empty save for me and the whispering women. There was just nobody would take me.'

Ruth found herself wanting to murmur compassionately but she was unable to make a sound. Her eyes were sombre as Tommony went on, 'I remember thinking to myself, nobody wants me – not even my Mammy and Pappy because it was they who'd sent me away. I was so miserable I wondered if I could slip outside when no one was looking and find my way back home. See, I didn't understand then that it was because I was black nobody wanted me. I thought it must be because these whispering women – I'd got to hate them by now – were telling everyone lies about me having done something wicked. Then this woman came in. She looked nice and kind of smiley. Comfortable, sort of, and easy – a bit like my own Mammy but white-skinned. I didn't think she'd want me any more than all the others had wanted me and by this time my mouth wouldn't smile for me any more. The women started whispering at her and I wanted to cry out to her, "It's not true what they're telling you! I'm not wicked!" But I didn't need to. She just pushed them aside and hurried up to me with a big smile on her face. "So here's the little boy I've been looking for," she said. "Tommony they call you, do they? Well, Tommony, I'm sorry I took so long coming for you." She had me by the hand and was sweeping past those women as if they weren't there and she took me off to her home and made me right welcome. Oh, she was grand was Aunty Flo. That's what I used to call her.' His voice shook a little and he smote a fist into his palm. 'That's my main memory of the war,' he said.

Ruth smarted with humiliation, suspecting that, faced with similar circumstances, her own mother would have been among the rejectors. 'Were you happy with this woman?' she asked.

'Oh, sure. Happy enough. She was real good to me. But there's another bit of the story that you should know,' Tommony continued. 'Aunty Flo was a widow

119

and found money pretty tight; mostly I think because she was a bit happy-go-lucky and not too wise at managing the housekeeping. Anywise, when she was helping me undress that night she found sewn inside my vest a five-pound note along with a letter from my Mammy saying, "Whoever takes care of this child and is kind to him will get more of these." ' Tommony gave a grunt of satisfaction. 'Five-pound notes were worth a good deal more in those days than they are now and when she saw this one – I can still remember how she unfolded it and held it in her fingers, looking at it as if it had come there because of a conjuring trick – she had a little weep. I didn't know why she cried but when my folks came to see me she told them the five pounds had seemed like a miracle. That particular week, knowing she was expecting a child might be billeted on her, she'd spent the last of her pension and had nothing left to pay one or two bills that had come up.'

Tossie murmured a sleepy comment.

'Have you kept in touch with her?' Ruth queried.

'I did for a whiley,' Tommony said. 'Pretty regular at first. But then after the war she went to live with a married son in Canada. We wrote sometimes and then it was just a card at Christmas time and then they stopped coming so either she died or she forgot me. I only hope, whatever happened to her, folks were as kind to her as she was to me,' Tommony ended ruminatively.

Into the quiet of the night there came another burst of gunfire, sounding even more distant than the first but still menacing enough to make Ruth cringe.

'Tossie hasn't heard that,' Tommony whispered after a short pause. 'She's fast asleep, thank God!' They listened for more sounds of combat but when some time had elapsed without the silence being broken Tommony began to speak with quiet urgency. 'Ruthie, no matter how Tossie feels about it, I've got to go at first light and see where's the best place to make for. We can't keep on the way we've been. It's senseless trying to get to places and then having to turn back. That way we're going to be out of petrol and still not getting any place.'

Ruth baulked at the idea of his leaving them, even temporarily, but she knew he spoke wisely. 'Yes, I understand that, Tommony,' she whispered back.

'Let's hope Tossie will stay sleeping when I have to go,' he said.

'It might be as well,' Ruth agreed. 'I can do the explaining if she wakes before you get back.'

The eastern sky paled as dawn inched its way over the hill. Tossie and the children were still sleeping when Tommony rose.

'Keep your stick by you, Ruthie,' he mouthed soundlessly, using his hands to enact his words. 'Wake Tossie if anything moves. I'll give three short whistles when I come back so you'll know it's me.' They exchanged tacit nods before he turned and crept stealthily away.

Ruth sat rigidly, her body so charged for action her nerve ends felt live enough to be emitting sparks. Staring ahead into the half light her eyes strained to detect any movement. Senses she had forgotten she had now reasserted themselves, heightened by a tyranny of fear that opened her ears even to the sibilance of the morning air stirring the grass and the faint rustlings of tiny animals among the undergrowth. She could smell the elusive smell of crushed bracken newly washed with dew. She was so perceptive she felt she would be able to smell the approach of an enemy.

While she kept her solitary vigil the hazards of her mission flogged her mind, interlaced with visions of what new dilemmas might possibly confront her. Supposing a situation arose where she could save only one child? Supposing she herself might become a victim

121

thus leaving the children unprotected? The agony of such thinking made her want to cry out; to bury her head in her hands and shut out the torturous train of thought. But she dare not. She must stay constantly on the alert.

A slight stirring in the tent was followed by the appearance of Simon beside her.

'Where's Tommony?' he asked in a hushed whisper.

'Gone to reconnoitre,' she replied, slipping an arm around his shoulder.

'I hope he gets back all right,' Simon said fervently. 'It's nice having him with us, isn't it, Mummy? He's looking after us, isn't he?'

'I pray he will,' Ruth said briefly.

Simon leaned close to peer into her ravaged face. 'Has anything happened while I've been asleep?' he asked.

She hesitated. 'A couple of bursts of gunfire,' she disclosed. 'Tommony said it was a long way away. No need to worry about it.'

'Gunfire?' He spoke with bated breath. 'There must still be some fighting then?'

'Must be,' she admitted. 'Simon,' she began tentatively. 'I don't want to frighten you but suppose anything should happen to me before we get to Granny's, you'd try to look after everyone, wouldn't you? Keep everyone together, I mean.'

'But if we're all together there's nothing can happen to you that won't happen to us, is there?' he reasoned.

'I'm talking about something that could possibly happen, darling. It's the remotest of remote possibilities but it just might. You see a bomb or a gun could perhaps kill me but no one else. I know it's a terrible responsibility but I'd just like to know you'd do your best. You see what I mean, Simon?' She squeezed his shoulders.

'You didn't have to ask,' he said huffily and turned away.

'I know that really,' she told him. 'But I'm in such a state I'm afraid to trust even myself.' She hugged him again and for a few minutes neither of them spoke. Then Simon asked, 'How long has Tommony been gone?'

'I can't say,' she replied. 'It was just getting light when he went so I suppose he's been gone now for about an hour. I hope he'll have found a way out for us. We neither of us have petrol to spare for following any more blind alleys.'

'We should be all right for petrol,' Simon pointed out. 'But motor bikes don't carry much fuel and Tommony's got a lot longer way to go than we have.'

'He is very likely carrying a spare can,' Ruth said.

'I'm pretty sure he isn't,' Simon said. He was quiet for a while and Ruth sensed he was uneasy about something. 'Has Tommony spoken to you about petrol?'

'Yes,' she confessed.

'Did you tell him we have a spare can in the brake?'

'No.'

'Why didn't you?'

'Because I was afraid he. . . .' She halted. 'Because I was afraid he might steal it from us and leave us without enough to get to Granny's.'

'But he wouldn't, would he? Tommony's kind.' Simon was shocked.

'He seems kind,' she corrected him defensively. 'But in crises even the kindest people change. We can't take the risk of trusting anyone too much; I can't anyway. Not when I'm responsible for the lives of you and the others. Tommony's desperate to get his family to safety and you must understand when people are desperate enough they do things they wouldn't think of doing at any other time. You heard Tommony himself say that

123

no one can afford pity when the situation is like it is now.'

Simon thought for a moment. 'If we were desperate would we steal from other people?' he asked. His clear, candid eyes held hers.

'But we're not desperate for petrol,' she hedged.

'But if we were?'

'Perhaps. It's not nice to think about what one might have to do,' she said evasively. He continued to regard her gravely, compelling her to continue. 'If other people had plenty and we, as you say, were really desperate the answer is, yes. I wouldn't think it was all that wrong to steal from them.'

'But if they didn't have plenty – only just enough for themselves and we were truly desperate?' he pressed.

In a flash she saw the import of his questioning. She met his eyes and they stared at each other with steady, comprehending sadness. 'I would stop at nothing to get you all to safety,' she acknowledged and held his shoulders even more tightly.

It was fully light before they heard Tommony signalling his return. 'I've struck lucky,' he announced, not troubling now to keep his voice low. 'I met up with a farmer who's going to help us. He was hiding from me, thinking I was one of the rebels, but his dog barked and gave him away. He said it's just himself and his wife at the farm and they've already had a visit from some of the "louts" as he called them. They weren't violent but they helped themselves to all the food they could lay their hands on. Anywise,' Tommony went on, 'this old fellow told me there's a track a little way further on. If we can get the brake and bike through a couple of fields first then we hit this track which goes under the railway instead of over it. A cattle arch, he called it and he reckons once we're through that there's only a couple more fields between us and the main road. He seems a nice chap,' he added. 'Said he would run his tractor through to clear the way a bit for us seeing the track hasn't been used for a while but then he remembered he hadn't any fuel.'

'I suppose he couldn't be after a chance to steal some of ours?' Ruth hinted.

Tommony shrugged. 'He's old,' he said.

'How do we get to his farm?' Ruth asked.

'Oh, easy enough,' he replied. 'We go back along here for a little way. Here, look! See that now? The old man had a stub of black pencil in his pocket but neither of us had any paper so he tried to draw the way for me on the back of my hand. Trouble is it doesn't show up too well, does it?' Tommony grinned good humouredly as he displayed the back of his hand. 'Needs a lighter background,' he said and his grin widened. 'I'll remember the way okay though.' He became suddenly confident. 'Now suppose we brew some coffee and wake Tossie?' But Tossie was on the verge of waking and began questioning and scolding when she found Tommony had deserted them while she had been sleeping.

'Did the old man have any news about the way things are going?' Ruth demanded as she got out the biscuits ready for the children's breakfasts.

'Not much,' Tommony replied. 'The radio was on for a little while this morning, he said, but it soon went dead again. All he heard was a warning to people to keep off main roads. But he said the rebels he met seemed pretty confident things were going their way. They told him they hadn't met with a lot of resistance.'

Ruth swallowed nervously. 'Let's wake the children and get on our way,' she said fervently.

10

At the same time as Ruth and Tommony and Tossie were keeping watch outside the tent where the children slept, *Moonwind*, still without lights, was sailing through the darkness towards the Cove. David and Clyde had decided that their best plan was to drop anchor fairly well out in the bay and for Clyde to stay with the boat while David went ashore to be reunited with his family and to assess the situation. There had been no news since the message from the coastguard but though the two men had thrashed anxiously over the possibility of the trouble having already spread beyond the Port they had not seriously envisaged a spot as remote as Jeannie's smallholding coming within the area of conflict. All the same they knew they must be prepared for such a contingency.

If when he arrived at Jeannie's David was doubtful about their remaining there then, under cover of darkness, he would bring his family down to the boat when they would set sail for the Anchorage which was as far as they could get away from the troubles. With this in mind, and guarding against possible treachery, they had taken the precaution of agreeing on a codeword by which they could identify each other when David returned. Meantime, to repel any unwelcome invaders, Clyde had ready on *Moonwind*'s deck a flare pistol with a good supply of flares. Such flares were intended for firing into the air as a signal of distress; fired directly at a close target they could be as lethal as a bullet.

'Okay?' they asked each other as David lowered himself into the dinghy. 'Okay!' they each responded.

There were no lights visible on the shore but then the

Cove was small and secluded; a narrow inlet between tumbled rocks with only a small tidal jetty where one could go alongside in a dinghy. David, choosing to avoid the jetty, beached the dinghy, dragging it up until it was partly concealed behind the rocks over which he had to scramble to reach the road up from the shore. As his feet gained the relative smoothness of the road a barked instruction to 'Halt!' cut through the darkness. David froze as the bright beam of a torch focused on his face and two heavily booted figures accosted him.

'What the Hell's happening?' David demanded, angry with himself for being so startled.

'Who are you?'

As the beam of the torch moved, David saw that a rifle was being pointed at his chest. He gave his name and then asked, 'Who the Hell are you?'

'Military!' they replied. 'What's your business here?'

'I'm on my way to my sister's place up in the hills,' he told them. 'My wife and children had to get out of the Port and I'm joining them up there.'

The soldiers conferred for a few moments in low voices, stil keeping David covered with the rifle.

'Look, what's all this fuss about?' David asked truculently.

The soldiers ignored his question. 'Where exactly is your sister's place?' one of them enquired and, when David had given the information, the man said, 'You must be the chap the policeman has been keeping a look-out for.'

'The police?' A tremendous dread plunged through David and he took an involuntary step forward. 'Tell me what's happened, for God's sake!' His voice burst harshly from his swelling throat.

'Keep back!' ordered the soldier with the rifle.

'Blast you! Will you tell me, please. Has something

happened to my family? Please. I'm begging you.' His hands went out in a gesture of appeal.

'It's no good asking us. We don't know a thing except that our orders are to notify the police as soon as you arrive.'

A sharp exclamation broke from David. His chest heaved. His body felt crippled with foreboding.

'You'd best come into the boatshed and we'll contact the policeman and tell him you're here,' the soldier continued and added more leniently, 'If you're the chap he's looking for he can take care of you himself.'

They escorted him to a dimly lit boatshed and told him to sit down on a plank of wood which rested across two oil-drums. The soldier with the rifle stood in front of him but the stock of the rifle was resting on the floor. Unseeingly, David stared straight in front of him, his body in the grip of such emotion he wondered how long he could stand the suspense.

When the policeman arrived the two soldiers moved back to stand by the door. David jumped up but before he could speak the policeman said, 'I have a message for you from your wife. She and the children are safe but they've had to leave your sister's place because the military were taking over the area. They're making for the Anchorage. Should be there now.'

David's relief was so intense it had the stunning effect of a blow. His family were safe! The words rejoiced through every fibre of his being. He covered his eyes as exultation replaced the torment of dread which had held his body.

'They left yesterday morning, as a matter of fact,' the policeman went on. 'Your wife and the three children and the dog,' he said with steady emphasis.

David looked up quickly. 'And my sister as well, I take it? Or had she left before they got there?'

The policeman's mouth tightened. 'Sit down again,' he suggested.

As he listened to what the policeman was telling him David became consumed first with horror and then with rage and finally with an abysmal sadness. His head sank forward into his hands but he made no sound. His fingers trembled as he dragged them away from his set, white face. 'Where is she now?' he asked dully.

'The mortuary,' the policeman replied.

Fighting against the weight of his sadness David rose to his feet. 'Is there anything to be done?' he asked.

'Nothing yet. I have your parents' address and they'll be contacted soon. There's nothing I know of to detain you here but,' he paused, 'there's another piece of bad news I have to break to you. Your home, The Braes. It's gone. They did well to get out when they did. Others weren't so lucky.'

David looked at him almost vacantly and then, squaring his shoulders, he made for the door. The two soldiers moved aside to let him pass.

The moon had disappeared behind a thick bank of cloud and a thin shower of rain was hissing on the water as David rowed out to *Moonwind*. He gave the codeword.

'Okay?' Clyde called eagerly.

'Okay!' David sounded surly.

'Say,' Clyde began when David was aboard, 'what happened back there? I saw a light moving. Did you meet anyone? Get any news?'

David said levelly, 'I met the local policeman. He had a message for me from Ruth. She and the children left Jeannie's yesterday for my parents' place at the Anchorage. This whole damned area has been commandeered by the military.' He went towards the wheelhouse. 'Come on, Clyde. Let's get away from here,' he added with hoarse urgency.

Clyde cut in quickly; 'Dave! You said Ruth and the children? Didn't Jeannie go with them? Surely

Jeannie's not alone up there, is she?' He made a swift movement as if he intended going immediately to seek out Jeannie.

'It's no use, Clyde.' David cleared his throat and spat into the sea.

'David!' Clyde's voice was tense. 'Jeannie's okay, isn't she?' When David was slow to reply he lunged forward and gripped his arm compellingly. 'For Christ's sake, man, tell me. Has something happened to Jeannie?'

David's reply came disjointedly. 'Ruth found her . . . dead . . . They'd. . . . There's nothing we can do. . . .' He pulled away from Clyde's arm. His voice broke and his body became convulsed with dry sobs.

'No!' Clyde's agonized denial was shouted at the night. 'No! No!' His clenched fists hit at the wheelhouse again and again. 'Oh, God!' he moaned. 'Oh, God!'

Moonwind swung to the rhythm of the sea as the two men stood grim-mouthed and glaring bitterly into the rain-misted darkness. At last Clyde said, 'Yeah, let's go, Dave. We sure will get right out of this bloody place. Right the way out!' Half-blinded by rage he bounded along the fifty-foot deck in his haste to get the anchor.

11

Wakened from their sleep the children, looking like a group of dishevelled little ghosts, stood close together silently watching the tent being dismantled and re-stowed in the back of the brake. Flimsy as it was they had accepted the tent as a protective shield and seeing it first slump and then finally collapse as the tent poles were removed made them feel bereft; as if a cosy coverlet had been snatched away on a cold night.

Ruth herself, despite her eagerness to get on with the journey, knew a moment of regret at leaving the camp site. The concealing bracken had provided a refuge and a pause for reflection and wound-licking; getting the brake back on the road entailed stiffening up her mental and physical resources yet again to withstand the poss-ible hazards of the rest of the journey. But at least, she comforted herself, this time they would not be starting out alone. Tommony and Tossie would be with them until shortly before they reached the main road and once across that she would be in familiar country.

An early morning mist was draping fine grey curtains over the hills and by the time they set off a thin, pin-like drizzle was falling, obscuring the windscreen yet not to the extent of needing the wipers to be on continu-ously. Ruth followed Tommony until they reached a dilapidated gateway where he stopped and prepared to dismount. Almost immediately a man appeared from behind the hedge as if he had been awaiting Tommony's arrival. Ruth watched him suspiciously but with a friendly wave the man dragged open the gate and beckoned Tommony to drive through. She followed more cautiously, swayed by the suspicion they might be running into a trap. Once the two vehicles were through the man dragged the gate shut again, propping it with broken pieces of itself. Watching him, Ruth thought the gate such a puny deterrent she wondered why he bothered.

Almost as if he had read her thoughts he came up to the brake and winking cannily said, 'A gate's a gate, Missus. When the troubles are over I can always say the military or the rebels were responsible for smashing it down and claim compensation.' The ugly thought flicked through Ruth's mind that there would be worse vultures already calculating their expected gains from the catastrophe, but the man's reasoning, as characteristic of a hard-working farmer as was his rosy, weather-worn face, dispelled her suspicions of a possible trap.

'Have you a telephone?' she asked him eagerly.

'We have. But they tell us we're not allowed to use it. "No civilian telephone calls." That's what they said when we tried. They said it pretty fierce too, as if they meant it. We've been wanting to get in touch with our daughter, but the last time we tried they told us we'd be traced and punished if we tried again.' He shook his head. 'I wouldn't durst let anyone near it,' he said emphatically.

'Is there any way of getting messages to people?' Ruth persisted.

'No way I know, save shanks's pony, Missus,' he told her.

Ruth thought for a few moments. 'If you are able to use the telephone again within the next few hours would you do something for me?' The man nodded and she gave him the telephone number of David's parents. 'Please will you tell them we're on our way and we should be with them soon. Just say it's a message from Ruth, will you, please?'

Producing a stub of pencil which was doubtless the one he had used to draw the route on Tommony's hand the man now pushed up the sleeve of his own jacket and noted the telephone number on his hairy wrist. 'I'll be sure to do that if I get the chance,' he promised. 'You can trust me to do what I can.'

She felt a sudden surge of gratefulness and called out to him, 'Are you short of tea or coffee? We can spare some, if you are.'

'Tea!' he almost spat. 'We had plenty in the house but those louts took the lot. Even tipped up the caddy and emptied it. I can make do myself with milk but tea's like life's blood to my old woman. She's moanin' and gaspin' back there like a parched hen.'

As Simon dived among the packages in the back of the brake and came up with an unopened packet of tea the old man's eyes glowed. 'I can give you milk for the children,' he offered in exchange. 'Just you wait on here while I go to the dairy.' But Tommony shook his head.

'Thanks all the same but I think we'd better push on, don't you, Ruthie?'

She nodded agreement, at the same time adding her thanks to his.

'Aye well, then, maybe it's best that way seeing the rain seems to be setting in for the day.' The rain was indeed becoming much heavier and as he pushed the packet of tea into his pocket he said, 'That old cattle arch might be a sight muddy. See, it doesn't dry out so well not getting the sun but there's an old haystack in the field nearby. You can help yourself to plenty of that if you need it to get the vehicles through.' After a few more last-minute directions he lumbered off towards the farmhouse.

'Okay?' Tommony asked preparing to mount his bike.

'Okay!' Ruth replied.

Bumping their vehicles across fields that were sheened with rain they eventually saw the track which should lead them to the cattle arch. It was rutted by tractors and scored by runnels of rain but by now they were inured to rough conditions. When they came in sight of the cattle arch the children managed a faint cheer but as they approached it Tommony signalled he was stopping. Getting off the bike he walked forward and then with arms flopping in a gesture of acute despair, he came back to the brake.

'Did he mention mud?' he asked ironically. 'I'll say there's mud! I reckon if we manage to get the bike through it we'll be lucky. There's no chance for the brake from the look of it.'

'He spoke about an old haystack,' Ruth reminded him.

'It'll take a lot of hay to cover that lot,' he said. He wiped the rain from his face with his sleeve.

'Then we could spread the tent on top of the hay. That would help, wouldn't it?'

'I suppose so,' he agreed without enthusiasm. He leaned wearily against the brake.

Ruth looked at him worriedly, recalling how cheerfully he had coped with their difficulties up to now. How undaunted he had been by the setbacks they had encountered. She blamed the rain for his wilting spirits but nevertheless his air of defeatism provoked her.

'Well, I'm not giving up without trying,' she told him. 'I'm going after that hay before the mud gets muddier. Come on, Tommony,' she coaxed. 'The sooner the better.'

Simon said, 'There's an old stone shed that's half collapsed back there. Maybe we could use some of the stone from that. I can carry pretty big stones.' His voice was eager. 'I helped Daddy get his car out of a ditch once,' he added knowledgeably.

'You did?' Tommony gave Simon a whimsical smile. Suddenly he recovered his spirits. 'Come on then, let's get busy.' He ran towards the hedge and looked over

134

it. 'Yes, there's the stack the fellow told us about. Just in the middle of the field here.'

Leaving the younger children in the brake out of the rain, Tossie and Ruth ran to and from the abandoned stack, pulling heavy armfuls of the rotting hay and spreading it over the mud. After carrying a few sizeable stones Tommony and Simon, perceiving that the hay might be effective on its own, joined the two women, pulling hay recklessly from the stack, spreading it lavishly and then treading it until the mud was covered by a thick dung-coloured mattress. Sodden, bedraggled and muddied to the knees, they paused every now and then to gain breath and ponder how soon their efforts could be put to the test. When they judged it safe Tommony started the engine of his bike.

'Pray!' he exhorted them. 'Pray and keep your fingers crossed at the same time.'

The bike moved forward and there was a yelp of relief when, after a couple of waverings and whinings of the engine, it was safely across on to dry land. Giving the 'thumbs up' sign Tommony came with leaping strides across the hay. 'I reckon you're going to make it okay, Ruthie,' he encouraged. 'Tossie and me and Simon can push from behind to help.'

Tentatively Ruth revved the engine of the brake. 'Steady now!' called Tommony. 'Not too fast. Take it nice and easy, now.' The brake ground forward and then surged as the wheels gripped firm ground. Almost dizzy with relief Ruth got out. 'We've done it,' rejoiced Tommony. 'We've done it and we've got another black fellow here to prove it.' He pointed to Simon who had pushed with such vigour that when the brake had surged forward he had fallen flat on his face in the churned-up mud it had thrown out. With a rueful smile at his mother he began pulling handfuls of wet grass to wipe his face and hands.

Tommony again led the way along the margins of

two more fields and then they were crunching over sharp loose flints which clanged against the underside of the brake. The flinty road gave way to a smoother surface and after only a short distance the road forked. Here Tommony stopped the bike and dismounting came to speak to Ruth.

'According to the farmer the main road's only about a quarter of a mile away from here,' he told her. 'When you get to it, drive along it for about a hundred yards until you come to a turning on your left. That way, the old man reckons, you'll cut at least a couple of miles off your journey and you're more likely to be on safer roads.'

Ruth repeated his directions, wedging them firmly into her mind.

'What about you, Tommony?' she asked.

'We don't need to cross the main road now,' he replied. 'Where you fork left here, we fork right. Then, the farmer says, if we take the first turning after we've rounded the bend in the road we're on the right way. We just keep going, according to him.'

A dismal panic threatened Ruth. She would be on her own again. 'We part company here, then,' she said wanly.

'Guess so,' said Tommony.

She came to a sudden decision. 'How are you off for petrol, Tommony?'

He shrugged his shoulders, 'Well, unless we can beg, borrow or steal, I reckon we'll be hoofing it before long,' he admitted glumly.

'We have a spare can,' she told him. 'I'll need to top up the tank a bit but there should be some left.'

Tommony darted her a shrewd glance. 'That's great,' he said.

She was tense as she got out the can of petrol, fearful even now that his need might tempt him to treachery. Pretending not to see his hand outstretched to relieve her of its weight she struggled to lift the can. He unscrewed the filler cap and putting a hand under the can helped her tilt it. She relinquished her hold.

'Say when,' Tommony invited and before the fuel gauge had crept up more than a fraction she held up her hand, certain they had plenty of fuel whatever happened.

Tommony's face brightened as he tested the weight of the can and estimated the quantity of petrol. 'I reckon if all goes well we'll have enough here to see us there and half way back,' he gloated. Holding out his hand he said, 'Thanks a lot, Ruthie. And good luck to you and to all you kids there.' He grinned at the children. 'Maybe we'll all meet up again somewhere some day.'

Ruth grasped his hand. 'Thank you, Tommony. I honestly don't know how I would have managed without you and Tossie.' She found herself fighting against tears. 'Send me a card telling me you're all right,' she said as lightly as she could.

'Sure, and you do the same for me and Tossie,' he responded. They exchanged addresses.

'Marriott, your surname is, isn't it?' Ruth queried. 'Tommony Marriott?'

'Not Tommony on a postcard,' he demurred. 'Just plain "Tom". Tom Marriott.'

'Not Tommony? I did think it sounded a little unusual,' Ruth confessed.

'Ah well, see, it was thiswise,' he explained. 'I had a twin sister once and she was always known as "Honey". When Mammy called us it was always "Tom 'n' Honey". When my sister died – she was three at the time – I'd got so used to hearing "Tom 'n' Honey" I just didn't answer to plain "Tom". That's how I got to be "Tommony" and that's what I am today to everybody that knows me.'

'Well, goodbye, Tommony, and it's been good to know you,' Ruth said warmly.

'If you can come and say goodbye to Tossie and the kids,' he suggested. 'See it's a bit of a struggle getting out when the hood's up over the sidecar, particularly when we don't know how quickly we might have to get back in.' Tommony's eyes swivelled from left to right, emphasizing the need for alertness.

'God bless you all.' Ruth and Tossie gripped hands. 'Goodbye and safe journey.'

The children called their own goodbyes to one another as Tommony remounted his bike. Their hands waved from the open windows of the brake and that Tossie's children were responding was evident from the bouncing of the sidecar. Ruth thought she could hear Tommony's expostulations above the roar of the engine.

'They've gone!' announced Simon as the bike rounded the bend and disappeared from sight.

'Yes,' she acknowledged. 'We're on our own again now.' Bracing herself against useless regret she started the brake and took the left fork of the road. Someday, no doubt, she would be able to thumb over the memory of her encounter with Tommony and Tossie and their necessary companionship which had grown into comradeship and trust. Someday; perhaps quite soon. But not yet, her mind reiterated. She must defer such reflection until they were all safely at her parents-in-law's home.

'Once we're across the main road it's not so far to Granny's, is it, Mummy?' There was sharp expectancy in Simon's voice.

'No, not far. It shouldn't take us long now,' she confirmed and as the children exclaimed thankfully she was aware of a slight boosting of her own low spirits. But even as they came in sight of the main road they saw their way blocked by a group of stationary army lorries surrounded by soldiers.

Fear held Ruth in her seat as what she took to be an officer accompanied by two soldiers with rifles at the ready strode towards the brake.

'You can't go any further, madam,' the officer said authoritatively.

'But I need to get across the main road,' she protested.

He shook his head. 'No way. No one's allowed to take a vehicle on the main road.' He stood impassively beside the brake, the rain dripping off his helmet.

'But I shall only be on the main road for about a hundred yards,' she argued desperately. 'I take the first turning off to the left. I'd hardly be on the main road for two minutes.'

His glance wavered only to take in the children. 'Where are you making for?' he asked and when she told him he said, 'Hmm. About fifteen miles roughly. Well, the only way I can help is to get you and the children escorted across the main road on foot. I'm afraid you'll have to leave your vehicle behind for the time being. And don't lock it,' he advised. 'We might have to move it somewhere else.'

His words left her stupefied. 'Oh, please,' she cried when she could find her voice again. 'How can I possibly walk the children fifteen miles before dark?' There was sympathy in the eyes of the soldiers but the officer remained obdurate.

'Sorry, madam,' he said. As he moved away she heard him calling to a group of soldiers. One of the attendant soldiers who were still guarding the brake stepped forward. Ruth looked up at him dejectedly.

'To tell you the truth, madam, you wouldn't be able to get as far as the turning you want. The road this side of it was mined last night. One of our lorries was blown up.' He spoke out of the side of his mouth and glanced warily over his shoulder.

'Mined?' It was a moment before she grasped what he was saying.

'Seven of our lads copped it.' He looked blankly into the distance. 'A good thing you didn't get this far last night and try to cross. You might have been the one to trigger it off,' he added meaningly. A cold arrow of fear shot through Ruth as she listened. 'I shouldn't be telling you all this by rights,' he whispered before he moved back smartly as he saw the officer returning.

'Two of my men are ready to escort you across the road and put you on the right track,' he said, opening the door of the brake decisively and waiting while they got out. 'Take anything valuable or anything you're likely to want with you,' he instructed.

'My Gruntly's valuable,' Susan told him. 'He's got a gold ear-ring.'

'My penguin's valuable too,' claimed Heather.

'I'm taking my stick and my torch,' Simon announced.

'There's a sensible lad,' the officer complimented him. 'I wish some of my men were as bright as you.' He turned to Ruth who was sorting out anoraks and stuffing spare clothes along with the box of Jeannie's mementoes into a plastic bag. 'We reckon we've got the insurgents pretty well bottled up over this side so you shouldn't have much to worry about. All the same,' he went on, 'I'd advise you to keep to the woods and lanes as far as possible. There's always more risk of the odd incident when there's any sort of decent road.' His expression softened as he looked down at the dismal little party standing in the rain; his voice took on a tone of gentle apology. 'I'm just sorry there's nothing more I can do for you,' he said. As their escorts led them away he saluted. 'Good luck!' he called.

12

Once they had seen them safely across the road and had pointed out the path, their escort, after presenting each of the children with a bar of chocolate, bade them farewell. Ruth led the way and for a time the children were too preoccupied with their chocolate and in discussing what they had heard about the blown-up lorry to grumble that they were having to walk too quickly to keep up with her. When the chocolate had been eaten and the subject of the mined road had been picked to exaggerated pieces and discarded, they were soon demanding to know how long it was going to take to walk all the way to Granny's.

'Oh, darlings!' Ruth sighed contritely. 'I just can't say. Much will depend on how far Susan can walk between rests.'

'I'm ever such a good walker,' claimed Susan. 'But Gruntly's tired already so please can he have a rest in your bag?' Ruth added the teddy bear to her crammed bag.

At first when she had got out of the brake Ruth had felt her knees shaking treacherously but she had dismissed it as only a passing weakness. So fiercely had her protective instinct manifested itself she did not doubt her new-found strength would support her at least until the children were safe.

Asking Simon to take Heather's hand while she took Susan's, Ruth urged the children along the path towards the shelter of the trees. But the intricacies of the woods added to her unease as did their stillness which today seemed to be intensified by the constant sizzling of rain through the leafy branches. Doggedly they continued along the path.

'Five miles an hour is reckoned to be good walking,' Simon said. 'If we can take turns piggybacking Susan, it shouldn't take us more than three hours to get to the Anchorage.'

To Ruth his reckoning sounded over-optimistic but she felt it wiser not to comment, taking the attitude that if the children thought they could walk the distance in that time they might conceivably do so whereas a doubt cast now would weaken their resolve from the outset. But despite all her urgings their progress was dishearteningly slow, dragging to frequent stops. Their anoraks were soaked; the strap of Susan's sandal had broken causing her to limp along or else go barefoot when Ruth tired of carrying her; Heather was murmuring tearful warnings that her legs were going to drop off if she couldn't stop and rest them for a while.

Ruth had no idea of how far they had come or what time it might be, and looking up at the leaden sky which seemed to be pressing down on the tree tops she found little to help her. She judged it to be late afternoon since the hold-up at the cattle arch must have accounted for the greater part of the morning but there was no sun by which she could estimate the time. Nor, since her stomach was too numb to recognize them, was she able to approximate the odd pang of hunger to an hour of the day.

'Yes, I think we must take a rest,' she agreed. She put down Susan who she had been piggybacking herself for the last half hour. 'I daresay we shall get on a lot quicker after we've had a rest. I'm afraid there doesn't appear to be a dry place for us to sit,' she observed. 'We'll just have to make do with the wet ground.' They were already so wet they couldn't get any wetter, she told herself, and anyway sitting on wet ground was a small enough risk when compared with those they had already come through unscathed.

The children flopped to the ground thankfully only raising their voices to protest when Tansy came and shook herself close beside them. Lying back, they tried screwing up their eyes and puckering their mouths against the onslaught of the rain and when that proved no protection they turned over on to their stomachs and hid their faces in the grass. Ruth slipped off her anorak and spread it over the two girls, then, reaching for Simon's stick, she too sat down, calling Tansy to come and keep watch beside her.

The children continued to lie quietly as if they were sleeping but Ruth remained alert, blinking the rain from her eyes and keeping her ears attuned to detect the slightest sound while she peered into the hissing gloom. She tried to calculate how far they might get before darkness set in; what they would do when it got dark? Undoubtedly darkness would aggravate not only the children's fears but her own. It would make it more difficult to keep a close eye on her children and though they had Simon's torch she wondered if, in the circumstances, it would be wise to use it. Reluctantly she came to the conclusion that they must soon begin keeping their eyes open for some shelter for the night.

Her mind switched to the farmer and she mused on whether he had been able to get a message to her in-laws. Her thoughts swung to David on *Moonwind*, tracing his likely progress. On receiving the coastguard's message he would have made straight for the Cove. At the Cove the policeman would have directed him to the Anchorage. Arriving there – supposing he had arrived – and not finding her and the children, he and Clyde would have immediately set out to search for them. Assuming their search had brought them to the military road block then they would have learned how she and the children had been ordered to abandon the brake and proceed on foot. They would have been shown the route to follow. They might even now be in the vicinity! Hope dared to raise itself on tip-toe. At any moment now David might emerge from the screen of rain! In her weakened state so vividly did she imagine him searching the woods that she strained to hear his voice calling to her from among the trees. But the rain muffled all sound save its own doleful rustling and dripping.

When she thought they were sufficiently rested she roused the children and seeing how shivery and befuddled they were she hurried them along, promising that hurrying would soon make them warm again. But though Simon and Heather stoically refrained from grumbling about their weariness, Susan kept up a woeful alternation of complaints and entreaties which even her mother's feigned indifference failed to discourage. As the gloomy day wore on to an even gloomier evening the children were again slumping and stumbling with fatigue and try as she could Ruth could not whip their flagging spirits.

'It's no use,' she told them forlornly. 'We must try to find some shelter for the night.'

Heather hugged herself. 'We should have brought the tent with us,' she criticized.

'I couldn't have carried the tent and this bag and piggybacked Susan, could I?' Ruth reasoned testily.

They were out of the woods now and making their way along leafy lanes while they peered through the obscurity of the dusk for some likely shelter. They came upon a high stone wall which looked as if it might be a bridge but on investigation they discovered a door in the wall – a discreet but solid-looking door, set deep and with a rusty iron ring that looked as if it might be a handle.

'It could be the door to an old shed or somewhere,' Simon suggested and before Ruth could caution him he had grasped the handle and was struggling to turn it. But the ring was rough with rust and refused to yield even the fraction of an inch. Simon kicked at the door. 'If I could stand on your shoulders I might be able to climb up and see if there are any lights showing on the other side,' he suggested.

'I don't think we should,' Ruth said dubiously. 'Just let's try looking around a bit more before we do anything like that.'

'I don't want you to open that door!' Susan cried out in sudden panic. 'I think it's the door into a witch's den.'

Before she had finished exclaiming they all heard the sound of a heavy bolt being drawn and as the door creaked ponderously open a tall, dark-cloaked and hooded figure carrying a hurricane lamp stood before them. Susan gripped Ruth's neck so tightly it was nearly unbearable while Heather pressed close against her thigh almost disabling her. Ruth vaguely recalled having heard of some strange religious sect which was reputed to have taken a house not far from the Anchorage. She suspected they might have stumbled upon it.

'Who's that kicking at this door?' The voice was aggressive, the accent strongly Irish. There was a pause which Tansy filled with irresolute growls. The hurricane lamp was lifted higher. 'Dear God Almighty! What have we here? Is it children you are, for Christ's sake! And if you are, what in Christ's name are you about on such a night?' The voice was gruff enough to be male but the tone of concern led Ruth to judge it to be female. She swallowed nervously.

'There are three children and myself and our dog,' she said. 'We're on our way to the Anchorage. We left the Port yesterday morning. I expect you've heard it suffered badly from an attack. We had to abandon our car and we've been walking since then. We're all wet through and the children are tired out. We were just trying to find some sort of shelter from the rain.'

'Saints alive! Is it these prowling villains who've driven you to such a state? Ah, but you poor lost souls. You'll not make the Anchorage this night for it's another eight miles from here.' She swung the lamp, letting its light waver over them. Ruth felt there was no malice in its beam. Even Tansy appeared satisfied that the figure was not to be mistrusted. 'You poor, drownded angels,' the voice commiserated. 'Just you follow me now into the house. Indeed I'd be a poor lost soul myself if I couldn't find you food and shelter for the night.'

Ruth felt Susan squirm against her but to her the solicitude had sounded convincingly genuine and she stepped through the doorway. The children followed and the woman bolted the door. 'This way, my darlings,' she said and led them through a narrow, shrub-bordered path towards the back premises of a fairly large house. An easily detectable smell of whisky trailed behind her as they followed her down several stone steps and through a second heavy door into a large kitchen where a glowing fire burned enthusiastically in an enormous old-fashioned cooking range and a pressure lamp stood on a solid-looking, green-painted dresser.

'There now!' said the woman, divesting herself of the bulky black cape and black plastic pixie hat which had accounted for her cloaked and hooded appearance. 'Come and warm yourselves.'

The children hung back, gazing at the woman with eyes that spoke their distrust. Ruth appraised the woman quickly. She was stocky in build but the abundance of crimped black hair piled high on her head gave her the appearance of being taller. Her long, full-skirted dress was an ageing black but the capacious apron which covered it was a snowy white. Her rolled-

146

up sleeves showed forearms that were wrinkled and splodged with pale brown spots like the foxing on an old print. Her eyes were treacle black, the whites looking dingy brown and her cheeks had ruddy patches that paled as they reached her mouth.

'Come, come now,' coaxed the woman, smiling at the children. 'It's not afraid of me you are, surely?'

'Yes,' volunteered Susan timorously. Ruth squeezed the child's hand and drew it more firmly into hers.

'Wait you then, me little darlin', till you see what I'm going to do for you. First I'm going to get you some nice warm blankets so you can wrap yourselves up while we dry out your clothes on the rack above the fire. Next I'm going to get you something nice to eat, for sure, you must be near starving, and then,' she clapped her hands, 'and then I'll maybe tell you some of the stories my Mammy used to tell me when I was little, just like you. What would you think of that now?'

Susan managed a twitch of a smile. 'What sort of stories? Would they be about witches?'

'No indeed, not about witches but about wee leprechauns and gentle giants and nice kind fairies that lived up on the hills in Ireland. Would you have a fancy for that now, my little darlin'?'

Susan appeared to be reassured but Simon and Heather were still regarding her with suspicion when she blew them a kiss before disappearing through a door at the far end of the kitchen.

'D'you think we're going to be safe here, Mummy?' Heather whispered through chattering teeth.

Ruth looked down at her troubled face. 'Yes,' she committed herself, praying she had given the right answer.

When the woman returned she was almost hidden under armloads of blankets.

'Here you are now, me darlin's. Get those wet clothes off you and wrap these blankets round yourselves. And

147

get you closer to the fire,' she added. The children glanced at Ruth, awaiting her approval, and when she nodded they plucked up courage and moving nearer the fire began to take off their clothes. Susan started to undress herself but when coaxed submitted to sitting on the woman's lap and being helped off with her clothes.

'Now, tell me, what name shall I call you by, little one? That is if you have a name at all,' the woman teased.

'Of course I've got a name,' Susan retorted. 'My name's Susan.'

'Ah, Susan! Hear that now. A pretty name for a sweet pretty girl.' She stroked the child's hair. 'And your hair is soft as a fairy's and smells as fresh as the purest mountain dew.'

Susan spared her a critical look. 'You haven't told me your name yet,' she taxed her.

'My name? Why everyone calls me Cookie.'

'Cookie?' echoed Susan. 'I think that's a very funny name.' She knelt so as to sniff at the woman's hair. 'And I don't think your hair smells very nice at all,' she said candidly.

'I'm Cookie because I do all the cooking here. Or I used to when the family were here. What else would anyone call me?'

Ruth, fearing a further blunt reply from Susan, interposed. 'You're lucky to have a coal-fired range. I don't suppose the electricity is back on again yet.'

'Lucky? Didn't I swear to them I'd take myself back to Ireland the day they'd take out this old range and give me electrics? And I was right, was I not? If the family had been at home this past day or two they'd have been missing their hot dinners if I hadn't had my way about the old range. Oh, yes, they would have had cause to be thankful to old Cookie.' She pulled the blanket around Susan and cradled her in her arms.

'Anyway,' she went on, 'I'm one that likes to see a bit of a blaze of an evening, summer or winter, for this is a biggish house and there's plenty of cold sneaking around it looking for old bones to chill into their graves.' She looked tenderly down at Susan who was now nestling trustingly against her bosom. 'Ah, but you remind me of a little girl who once lived here in this very house. A real sprite of a wee girl she was too.'

'Where is she now?' Susan wanted to know.

'The truth is she was taken. The Lord Jesus took her and broke her mother's heart,' Cookie lamented. 'There've been no children to liven up the house since and there'll be none any more I fear, though the nursery upstairs stays just the way it was on the day she died. Her mother wouldn't have a thing changed.'

At this moment Susan decided to wriggle off Cookie's knee and crouch with Simon and Heather on the hearthrug. Cookie stood up.

'Ah, but I mustn't make you all sad,' she said. 'There's sadness enough in the world without me adding to it. Come on,' she invited. 'Give me all those wet clothes. There's a good drying rack above your heads that's waiting to be filled.' She and Ruth gathered up the clothes and threw them over the rack. 'And this rack's another thing I've cause to be thankful for. A fat lot of use one of these tumble driers would be with no electric.'

'Are you here alone then?' Ruth asked.

'I am indeed. The family's been away in foreign parts off and on ever since the child died. The way things are going in this country there's little to tempt them back.'

'Have you seen any signs of the rebels around here?' Ruth found herself asking the dreaded question.

'Have I not indeed?' The note of derision in Cookie's voice made Ruth glance at her in astonishment. 'Oh, yes indeed, I've met some of the rebels as you call

149

them, though that's too easy a name for them I'd say. Did I not have three of them here not last night but the night before? Three young lads they were and all as drunk as newts. They come thumping on that door there, though I do believe they'd fallen down the steps to get to it.'

'Weren't you frightened here all by yourself?'

'Not me,' boasted Cookie. 'I slip a full bottle of whisky into the pocket of my skirt ready to crown them with it if I need to and then I open the door and I says to them, all friendly, "Good evenin' to you, gentlemen, and will you not come into my kitchen." ' She dissolved into hiccoughing laughter for a few moments. 'And then I make a deep, deep curtsey, just the way I'll show you now and by God! the minute they sees me didn't they fly up those steps as if they'd seen a ghost?' As she ended her account she burst into a shriek of whisky-fumed laughter and, turning to Ruth, made an exaggerated curtsey. At the same time she raised her hand and swiftly whipping off her pile of crimped black hair revealed a head that was totally, shinily bald. Ruth stifled a gasp as through her mind flashed the conviction that Cookie was a man in disguise. She stepped back, her glance going quickly to where her Tommony stick was leaning against a chair. The children gaped at Cookie while she, obviously enjoying their consternation, twirled the wig round and round on one finger. 'Would you not be scared out of your wits now to see someone take off their head in front of your eyes?' she teased. 'Sure, but that's what the brave heroes thought had happened, they were that drunk,' she explained. 'Drunken cowards they were and nothing but that,' she ended contemptuously. She rammed the wig back on her head somewhat crookedly and the children, who at first had been shocked at the sight of her bald head, now turned to one another with furtive smiles.

150

Going to one of the cupboards which lined the kitchen Cookie took out a half-full bottle of whisky and two glasses. Filling both she offered one to Ruth.

Ruth shook her head. 'Thank you, but no,' and when Cookie wanted to insist she gestured her away. 'I couldn't touch it at the moment,' she declined.

'Ah, come on now, girl. It's just what you need and there's plenty more where this came from. I'm telling you the old master has a cellarful down there and nobody here to drink it. By Jesus I'm telling you it's myself will drink the lot before I'll let it get into the wrong hands.' She proffered the glass again to Ruth but again Ruth shook her head. The smell of Cookie's breath was almost overpowering enough to make her feel queasy and she dared not risk allowing even a mouthful of whisky to flay her martyred stomach. Cookie shook her head regretfully. 'And I suppose you'll not even allow a wee teaspoon for the children,' she advocated. 'Sure it would take the chill out of them.'

'It's not all that cold,' Ruth demurred. 'They got cold from the rain but they should warm up quickly now. Anyway, whisky wouldn't be good for them on empty stomachs and they've had nothing to speak of in the way of food since yesterday morning.'

'For the love of Christ!' expostulated Cookie. 'What am I doing pouring whisky into my own stomach before I've filled their little stomachs? Shame on me indeed!' she castigated herself, at the same time as drinking both glasses of whisky and refilling her own glass. Moving about the kitchen with unsteady haste she opened cupboards and drawers and put out plates and spoons on the bare wood table. 'There's soda bread,' she declared. 'That's mostly what I eat myself. And I've flour and I've milk and I've eggs. Will you tell me now,' she turned to the children with a mischievous smile, 'which of yous doesn't like pancakes?' The children's denials were enthusiastic. 'Right you then. Just you wait now and you're going to see the finest pancake-maker in the country at work,' she promised. Cocking a humorous eye at Ruth she got out the ingredients and began mixing them together in a bowl.

The hissing of the lamp had weakened to a whisper; its mantle had become pallid through lack of pumping so it was mostly the glow of the fire that was reflected on the children's faces as they watched Cookie's antics with the frying pan. Between pouring and tossing and sliding golden pancakes on to their plates Cookie fortified herself with gulp after gulp of whisky. The pancake tossing became wilder and wilder. Tansy feasted on dropped pancakes. The signs of strain cleared from the children's faces to be replaced by expressions of anticipation and excitement. Their laughter pealed out, jarring Ruth into a sharp awareness of how empty of their laughter had been the last twenty-four hours. It seemed an eternity since she had heard her children laugh and now the sound was sending a recognizable thrill through her overdriven body. Her eyes rested gratefully on the startling, whisky-pickled old crank who had not only given them shelter and warmth and food but who was now so patently succeeding, for the time being at least, in wresting the minds of the children away from the horror of their experiences. She fought back tears of gratitude, even managing a wisp of a smile to satisfy the children when they looked up at her as if begging her to share their amusement. But her own laughter was shackled; shackled so tightly she doubted if it would ever again break free.

When the children had eaten their fill of pancakes they were already beginning to fall asleep.

'There's beds a-plenty for them but I doubt they'll be aired,' said Cookie, draining the bottle of whisky into her glass. 'But there's also blankets a-plenty so you can please yourselves where you all sleep.'

'I think we'd all sooner sleep on the floor here,' said Ruth, determined they were not going to be separated.

Cookie spoke to Simon. 'If you're not too tired, my lad, you can come and help me get more blankets,' she said, beckoning him to follow her. Ruth waited by the door listening anxiously to their voices growing fainter and then louder again as they returned. When they came into the kitchen bearing blankets and pillows she was back in her seat.

'Please will you dry my penguin for me by the fire?' Heather pleaded sleepily. 'He got wet on top of Mummy's bag.'

'Sure I'll do that, my dear,' replied Cookie.

'And my Gruntly Finny,' Susan added. She got up and began searching in the bag. 'He's not here,' she wailed. 'Where's my Gruntly!' She began to cry.

Ruth searched the bag. 'I can't think what's happened to him,' she confessed. 'Gruntly and penguin were both in there. Are you sure you didn't take him out at all, Susan?'

'She took him out when we had that rest in the wood,' Heather said. 'I took penguin out too but I put him back. Susan must have forgotten to put Gruntly Finny back.'

Susan howled her admission as Ruth cradled her on her knee. Within a few minutes she had sobbed herself to sleep.

Once the children were bedded down satisfactorily Cookie, after checking the doors and windows were secured, settled herself in her rocking chair within handy reach of yet another full bottle of whisky. Ruth sat opposite to her in an ancient armchair whose springing was as mortifying as a fakir's bed. She shifted her position several times before Cookie got up and, going to a large chest beneath one of the windows, extricated a pile of cushions all garishly embroidered with cats of every description and colour.

153

'There now,' she said dropping them into Ruth's lap. 'See if some of Flora's follies will give you comfort.' Ruth looked up enquiringly. 'She used to be housemaid here till she left to die,' Cookie explained. 'And cats and embroidery were her passions. I don't doubt but she's up in Heaven now persuading the angels to let her embroider cats on their wings for them, for she was a good woman.'

As she adjusted the cushions Ruth asked, 'Have you heard any news over the radio today?'

'Radio?' retorted Cookie disdainfully. 'Nothing but "Don't panic. The situation is in hand." But they don't tell you whose hand. More likely we've been taken over by that fellow whose voice always sounds as if it's been left out in the rain and got damp.' She heaved a scornful sigh. 'Dear God Almighty but I believe the same thing's happened to his brain.'

While they talked Ruth was aware of the frequency with which Cookie's hand was going towards the whisky bottle; of her conversation becoming so fuddled that she was unable to understand it. She was glad when it trailed into silence and Cookie, abandoning herself to her chair, closed her eyes. As she began to snore her head tilted and her wig began to slip until it covered one eye and exposed a margin of baldness above her left ear. Ruth was watching with fascinated awe when, in the middle of a snore, Cookie pulled herself upright.

'You's staring at me,' she accused almost truculently.

'No, no,' Ruth denied hastily. 'Or if I was it was because I was thinking to myself how much courage it must have taken to open the door when you knew there were rebels out there. They could have stormed their way inside.'

'If they were aiming to storm their way in they would have done it without waiting to have the door opened for them. And then like as not they'd have half killed and roasted me so I'd be having nothing to worry about now, would I?' Cookie responded nonchalantly. 'If they'd not done that,' she continued after another swig from the bottle, 'I would have plied them with a bottle of doctored whisky I have there in the cupboard.' Getting up she reeled towards the whisky cupboard and produced a similar-looking bottle to that already on the table. 'That's doctored whisky, though you'd never guess it from the look of it. My father showed me the way to do it at the time of the troubles. You can be nice to your enemy and then have him senseless in less than ten seconds after half a glass of this stuff.' She waved the bottle as if it was a flagpole. 'Then I would have had the brigands at my mercy,' she cried melodramatically.

'Yes, but what would you have done then?' Ruth pursued.

'Done? I would have dragged them one by one down to the well in the cellar and tumbled them into it. I took off the lid as a precaution in case I might be getting a visit from the likes of them.' She nodded meaningly.

'A well – in the cellar?' Ruth exclaimed. 'Is there water in it?'

'Sure there's water in it. A well wouldn't be a well without water now, would it? And good water it used to be when we used it, though that's not been for donkey's years.'

'Deep water?' Horror crept into Ruth's voice.

'Deep enough to drown a body,' Cookie replied blandly. 'Sure they'd not likely be missed neither with all the killings there've been.' With something that sounded like a chuckle she pushed her wig carelessly into position and sank back into her chair.

Ruth breathed normally again. 'There's no need for you to stay awake,' she volunteered. 'I've no desire to sleep so I'll keep watch and replenish the fire as it needs it.'

Cookie replied drowsily, 'Me? Sleep? Sure I never sleep, my dear. Not really sleep. I maybe doze every now and then but only with the help of the whisky. But these last six weeks and more I can't even shut an eyelid for the grief I have inside me.'

'You've lost someone dear to you?' Ruth probed compassionately.

'Is it dear, you say? More than dear but loved she was. I swear to Almighty God I loved her like she was my own child.' Cookie lifted the skirt of her dress and dabbed at her eyes. 'The farmer gave her to me when she was no more than a tiny piglet and I cosseted her and loved her for fourteen years to the day she lay down and died. Ah, me and my old sow we loved each other. Concepta I called her and she was almost human.' She looked across at Ruth. 'I daresay you are thinking it a funny thing that a cook would be keeping a pig, but the master said, seeing she was company for me, he didn't mind me having her so long as she didn't come into the kitchen. She did – but not when any of them were here, though she never misbehaved herself. Oh, she was a grand pig. She had brains and understanding and that's two things you wouldn't expect to find in most pigs now, would you?' Ruth shook her head. 'No doubt you'll be thinking I'm a sentimental old fool talking like this, but will you tell me now,' she looked steadily at Ruth, 'do you believe yourself that animals have souls and go to Heaven the same as ourselves when they die?'

'I do,' agreed Ruth, glancing down at Tansy.

'Me too,' asserted Cookie. 'And blasphemy though it might be I swear to you I pray to God Almighty every night since she died that he'll remember to see there's plenty of muck up there for my old sow to wallow in. Concepta was never one for green pastures.

No! Muck she was happy in and muck I pray she'll have.'

Hardly had Cookie finished speaking when her chin sank on her breast and less than a minute later she was again snoring loudly.

Ruth gave a small sigh of relief. Despite being on guard alone she felt easier now Cookie slept, there being a needling doubt in her mind that Cookie might not be the kindly eccentric she appeared to be; that they might be in a Hansel and Gretel kind of trap with Cookie turning out to be the wicked witch intent on luring them all to her dark cellar.

She watched and listened, keyed up to scent danger from wherever it might come. When the pressure lamp began popping repetitively, giving warning of its urgent need for paraffin, she sped to turn it off and when the fire needed stoking she did it with the utmost stealth, laying on each piece of coal with her bare hands lest the noise should disturb the old woman.

13

Ruth watched the dawn lightening the curtains. Furtively she drew them back and looked out. The rain had ceased but the trees and bushes still dripped their sad burden of raindrops and the shaggy lawns were a cheerless grey. She wondered whether she should wake the children so they could all get an early start but glancing at the clock she decided to let them have another hour of sleep. Doubtless they would make better progress for the extra hour's rest.

By the time they were stirring, the sunrise was being hurried on by frisky white clouds and a tentative wedge of sunlight was catching the rain-beaded grass.

With exaggerated yawns Cookie roused herself and immediately reached for the whisky bottle. Filling her glass she gulped the spirit down.

'Now,' she said. 'If you're sure you'll not take a drop I'll put the bottle away. It's just the morning and the night I like my drink. In the morning to wake me up and at night to put me to what sleep I can snatch.' She returned the bottle to the cupboard. 'Now for breakfast,' she announced. Producing a tin of corned beef she sliced it and heated it in a large pan along with the pancakes remaining from the previous evening. The children pronounced it to be delicious and ate heartily. Ruth managed to swallow only a few mouthfuls of tea.

'You should stay and rest yourselves for a while longer,' said Cookie persuasively.

Ruth was reaching for dry garments off the airing rack. 'No, my husband will be out looking for us by this time,' she said firmly. 'We expected to be at his mother's house by now.' She began rolling up the blankets they had used. 'We'll take these back for you if you'll show us the way,' she offered. 'There's quite a load of them to carry.'

'Right you are then, follow me,' Cookie accepted promptly and led them along a narrow passage which went into a broader passage and from there to a warren of small rooms which were obviously used for storage. 'Here we are then,' she announced as they entered a room lined from floor to ceiling with cupboards and deep drawers, two of which she pulled open. 'Just pop them in there, my darlings,' she instructed. She sighed. 'They'll likely not be needed again until the family's back.' She nodded towards a green baize door at the end of the broad passage. 'Beyond that there's all the grand rooms, covered in dust sheets, more's the pity.'

When they were ready to depart, Cookie, insisting they needed food for the journey, searched in various kitchen cupboards and produced a tin of Christmas shortbread and three tins of corned beef which she slipped into a strong nylon net carrier. 'I've mountains of the stuff,' she averred, waving away Ruth's protests. She handed the bag to Simon. 'You're a big strong boy so you can take care of that now, can you not?' Filling a bottle with water she gave it to Heather to carry. 'Now,' she said, 'wait you just one minute till I go down to the cellar and get you something better than water. No! No!' she held up her hand, silencing Ruth's objection. 'God Almighty knows I wish you a safe journey but there's no knowing what troubles you might still meet with. I'll be praying they'll be troubles that need no more than a glass of whisky to cure them.' She took a torch and swept out of the kitchen, soon to return with not one but three bottles of whisky cradled in her arms. Two of the bottles she put away in the cupboard, no doubt for her evening's consumption. The third one she handed to Ruth. 'Make sure and keep that by you, my dear,' she instructed. Ruth no longer tried to demur though she knew they already had too much to carry.

They said their warm thank yous and goodbyes, Simon and Heather shaking Cookie's hand gratefully.

'Come along, Susan,' Ruth said abstractedly. 'Come and say goodbye to Cookie and thank her for all her kindness.' An instant later she was on her feet. 'Susan!' she called crossly. 'Susan! Stop hiding and come here at once!' The other children stood appalled. Simon bent to look under the table in case Susan was hiding there. But Susan was not in the kitchen. Ruth tried to quell her mounting panic. It was impossible for anything to have happened to Susan. The outer door had not been opened and Ruth was completely certain that she had kept all her charges, including Tansy, constantly within her vision, her mind having conditioned itself to a mental counting of heads whenever they were not confined within the car. And yet, Susan, with her talent for disappearing, had managed to elude her at this critical time!

'She's still somewhere in the house, that's for sure,' declared Cookie.

'She was with us when we were taking the blankets back,' said Simon and rushed to the door of the passageway, where he called loudly for Susan. He turned to Ruth penitently as if he thought himself to blame. 'She must have lagged behind when we were comng back.'

'Well, she must be somewhere,' Heather observed. 'But I don't know where the "somewhere" is.'

They raced towards the storerooms, their calls echoing hollowly along the passageway.

'She must have heard us,' said Ruth and with her anger nourished by fear she began threatening Susan that she would be thoroughly smacked if she didn't show herself immediately. They stood, a forlorn group, looking at one another for inspiration. Ruth, catching sight of something in Cookie's expression, was suddenly at screaming point. 'The cellar! The well! You went down there! Did she follow you?'

Cookie's hand went to her throat. 'Pray God, she didn't,' she said devoutly and picking up the torch she hurried out of the kitchen with Ruth hard on her heels.

'Stay and keep an eye on Heather!' Ruth commanded when she found Simon following her. He was carrying his own torch and Ruth snatched it from him.

The heavy arched door of the cellar was half open. Ruth raced down the narrow stone steps into the darkness and flinging herself down by the well screamed Susan's name frenziedly into its dark depths.

'Surely to God the child would not have ventured down here on her own in the dark.' Cookie's voice cut into a stark interval of listening silence. 'Surely this would be no place to tempt a child?'

'Susan wouldn't have come here in the dark, Mummy,' asserted Simon who, though he had been told to stay with Heather, had chosen to believe that his mother had been too confused to know what she was saying. 'Susan's scared of the dark.'

Ruth's anguish lessened fractionally.

'I expect she's somewhere playing at dolls where she can't hear us,' Simon hazarded. 'She's always sneaking away and doing that,' he explained to Cookie.

'In that case likely as not she's slipped through that green baize door into the main hall and is pretending she's some grand lady,' said Cookie confidently. 'Come now and we'll see if I'm right.'

Still shaking with terror Ruth followed her towards the door which, when Cookie swung it open, revealed a spacious hall from the centre of which rose a wide staircase. With a yelp of recognition Tansy darted to the foot of the stairs where she stood looking up and wagging her tail. As they all raised their eyes a small exultant voice called, 'Mummy! Look at me!'

Wearing a drooping tutu, a tarnished tinsel head-band and pink ballet pumps, Susan stood poised on the top step smiling down at everyone and waving a wand from which trailed a few faded ribbons. 'Mummy! Don't I look just like the little girl on my birthday card?' she demanded to know.

'Susan!' Ruth's voice quavered as a flood of relief engulfed her. 'Susan!' she tried to scold, yet there was no asperity in her tone. She was about to run up the stairs but Cookie put out a restraining hand.

'Let the little darling have a few more minutes of pleasure,' she entreated. 'Did I not tell you that the nursery was left just the way it was on the day the daughter of the house died?' She called up to Susan, 'Come you down now, my little treasure. And it's your-self will be showing old Cookie what a good dancer you are before you leave me.'

They returned to the kitchen where Cookie found more biscuits. She brewed another pot of tea and after pouring out two cups she got up and began to 'la la' a tune while Susan danced. When Susan paused Cookie clapped encouragement and herself began gavotting around the kitchen.

Ruth could only pretend attention. The immensity of the relief from what she now knew to have been unnecessary panic was affecting her like an anaesthetic, and when Cookie pushed a cup of tea in front of her and proffered biscuits she took one absentmindedly, dunked it in the tea and put it into her mouth. It was the first food she had swallowed since leaving The Braes and her stomach, cringing at the assault, re-sharpened her senses.

'You'd best go out the same way as you came in,' advised Cookie, once Susan had changed back into her own clothes and they were ready to depart. She led them through the garden to the door in the wall.

'I hope you're going to be all right here by yourself,'

Ruth said. The thought of David and her confident expectation of being with him again in a very short time allowed her to consider the plight of others.

'Sure, why wouldn't I be all right?' Cookie responded. 'It's more than likely all the turmoil's over and forgotten by now anyway.' There was an insouciance about her that Ruth both envied and condemned. 'From the look of the fools I had here they shouldn't take much routing out.' She winked at Ruth. 'I've plenty of home comforts to keep me going till things are sorted out.' Her expression sobered. 'I pray God you'll be with your man before nightfall,' she said, 'you and the little ones.' She patted Simon's shoulder. 'You see and look after those tins of corned beef, young man. Corned beef puts strength into you, my father always used to say.'

They called their goodbyes once more as she stepped back through the doorway. The door slammed shut and they heard the noise of bolts being shot. They had gone only about two hundred yards beyond the house when they heard a shrill call and looking back they saw Cookie leaning out of an upstairs window. Her bald head shone in the sunlight and she was waving to them with what looked like a broomstick at the end of which was tied her frizzy black wig.

Simon looked up at his mother with a quizzical frown. 'D'you think she's a bit daft?' he asked.

'She was very kind to us,' Ruth said.

'She drinks a lot of whisky,' said Heather. 'It's a wonder she doesn't get drunk.'

Ruth made no comment.

Shelving the night's experience, Ruth's mind moved on to deal with the last leg of their journey. The grass was still wet from the rain and she urged the children on, wanting to get as far as they possibly could while the morning was still cool. But the children seemed even more sluggish than on the previous day and it was not long before the two younger ones were growing fretful, complaining they were sweating and begging to be allowed to stop for drinks and biscuits. She tried not to be affected by their growing resentment at what must have seemed to them her callousness in turning a deaf ear to their entreaties.

As the sun grew hotter there was little coolth even taking advantage of the shade provided by the tree-lined lanes. She knew she must allow the children to rest.

'We'll stop here and cool down just for a little while under the shade of this big tree,' she said. 'But then there can be no more rests until we get to Granny's. It's not very far now,' she encouraged. She stood flexing her cramped shoulders. Simon and Susan slumped thankfully on the ground but Heather confronted Ruth, lips pouting, eyes brimming with tears.

'I want to know why Daddy hasn't come for us yet,' she jerked out. 'You say it's not very far to Granny's and yet Daddy still hasn't come to find us. I think Daddy must be dead like Aunty Jeannie. I think he's been killed.' Flinging herself on the ground, she buried her face in the grass moaning piteously as spasms of grief shook her body.

'No!' As Ruth dropped down beside her she was aware of the faces of the other children stiffening with horror. 'No, darling,' she soothed, trying to take Heather in her arms but the child would not be comforted. Weighing her little body down on the grass and kicking her heels in protest she gave herself up to a torrent of weeping.

Helplessly Ruth looked at the others. 'Darlings, I'm sure Daddy's safe. I'm sure he's out looking for us even now this minute but we have to remember it's difficult for him to follow our tracks because we haven't been able to use the main road where he'd expect to find us. Please don't be upset. I'm sure Daddy's all right,' she reiterated and found herself fighting against a compulsion to repeat the phrase as if her voice had stuck like a needle in the groove of a record. The children received her assurances in a dejected silence.

Ruth called to Tansy to leave her hunting and come and lie down beside them, but as Tansy approached the tree under which they were resting she lifted her snout and sniffed suspiciously. A growl began to rumble in her throat and she bayed at something that was screened by the tangle of branches above their heads.

'What is it, Tansy?' Ruth shielded her eyes from the sun as she turned to look up, but before she could locate the object of Tansy's hostility an insupportable weight descended on her shoulders. As her knees buckled beneath her she was conscious of the terrified squeals of the children mingling with Tansy's savage yelping. She struggled violently but a hand held her throat like a vice and her head felt as if it were about to burst. She kicked out and tried to tear the hand from her throat but the pressure increased. With a shuddering moan she sank into unconsciousness.

When she saw the man attacking their mother, Susan ran away a few paces and then turned, watching the attacker and jumping up and down, shrilling her terror. Heather also took to her heels but, shocked by her desertion, she forced herself to return, venturing close to Simon who had made a brave rush forward to go to his mother's aid. Despite his own terror, despite his shaking limbs and the man's menacing threats and curses, Simon stood his ground, his hand clenching on the bag of corned beef tins he was carrying.

'Bite him, Tansy!' Heather found voice enough to yell at the little dog who, unbidden, was already savaging the man's ankles. Thus encouraged, Tansy intensified her attack, launching herself at the big clumsy man with all the savagery her lithe little body could summon. He swore and kicked out viciously against her but she was too quick for him. Blood oozed from his bare shins, blood dripped from his hand, and when he thrust out an arm to ward off her attack she nipped in smartly to spring at his face, tearing at his lip. When his hand went up to protect his face she leapt again and tore his ear. His gruff voice became high pitched with rage.

Meanwhile Simon's fingers were tightening on the nylon bag, drawing the neck up into a manageable handful as he moved towards the man's head. When the opportunity came he swung the bag and brought it down with every ounce of his strength on the back of the attacker's head. Expecting the man to turn on him he jumped back out of reach. He was surprised when the man only grunted and, gaining courage, Simon advanced cautiously and again swung the bag. This time there came a strange-sounding moan and the man's head fell forward to rest on Ruth's chest. With a feeling almost akin to elation Simon swung the bag yet again. The bag became stained with blood and there was blood on the back of the man's neck. He lay still and Tansy, ceasing her attack, was standing beside him, growling as if daring a vanquished opponent to resist. Simon heard his mother begin to gasp and hastened to loosen the man's hold on her. Fiercely protective, he sat beside her while her breath heaved itself back into her lungs.

'D'you think he's dead?' Heather came to kneel beside her mother.

Simon looked at the man who had rolled over on to his back. His eyes were closed. Simon looked away. 'No,' he replied. 'I only hit him hard enough to get him off Mummy and give us a chance to get away.' He looked challengingly at Heather. 'I wouldn't care if I had killed him,' he said.

'He was wicked, wasn't he? Really, truly wicked,' Heather said. 'I thought he was trying to kill Mummy.'

'I expect he would have done if I hadn't hit him with this,' Simon affirmed and looking disgustedly at the bloodstained bag he unclenched his fingers.

Susan would not come close to her mother until Ruth sat up and then she ran forward and clung to her desperately. Ruth gave them all only a brief hug before she managed to struggle to her feet. 'Let's get away as fast as we can,' she said, shrinking from even a glance at the prone figure. 'Come along. Please, very quickly. We must get away from here. You two hold on to each other,' she bade Simon and Heather, 'and I'll look after Susan. Run! Run!' They ran ahead but she herself was making such slow progress that they came back and took Susan between them. 'You'll be better without Susan,' they told her. 'We'll look after her, Mummy.' Even without Susan she could not keep up with them; her legs had become so feeble she expected them to collapse beneath her.

'Tansy's missing!' Simon shouted over his shoulder. He called her as he ran.

'Mummy, Tansy's missing!' repeated Heather.

Ruth managed to call and when Tansy did not appear she managed a shrieked repetition of her command. Glancing hastily over her shoulder she thought she caught a fleeting glimpse of the dog but she could not summon up the strength to call her again. She realized she had breath only to keep moving and to urge the children to greater speed.

14

When *Moonwind* had reached the Anchorage in the early hours of that morning, David, leaving Clyde in charge of the boat, had made straight for his parents' farm. Disturbed at finding no trace of Jeannie's brake near the house he had hastened round to the kitchen door, expecting to find it unlocked as always. But the door was securely fastened and he had had to hammer on it, at the same time as announcing himself in a loud voice, before his mother leaned out of the bedroom window. Within seconds she was unbolting the door.

'David!' she exclaimed, embracing him and drawing him into the kitchen.

'Ruth and the children? Are they here?' he asked urgently as he gave her a quick, strong hug. Her puzzled expression had answered him, bringing the remembered plunge of despair.

'Ruth and the children? Why no!' Her surprised eyes probed his. 'Are they on their way here?'

Quickly he explained what had happened, leaving out any mention of Jeannie. While he was doing so his father, slowed by a gammy leg, had joined them.

'Any petrol for the car, Dad?' David asked.

Immediately grasping the purport of the question his father replied, 'It would be no good to you if I had. I believe the main roads are closed except to the military. There's diesel for the tractors but you'd be far wiser to take your old bike. You'll likely get further on that than on a tractor.'

'Where is my old bike?' David was already half way out of the kitchen.

'In the tractor shed.' Hobbling after David, he

called, 'I'll make my way down to *Moonwind* so Clyde can come and help you look. That's something I'm still capable of doing. Herbie at the Post Office will be only too pleased to lend Clyde his bike.'

Eyes scanning the countryside David cycled on, dismounting frequently to explore tracks and cul-de-sacs where the brake might be hidden. By the time he reached the main road Clyde had caught up with him. Halted by the soldiers David's attitude was one of such desperation that Clyde feared for a moment he was on the point of rushing the barricade. The soldiers, similarly suspicious, stiffened to an extra degree of alertness.

Composing himself David explained, 'I'm looking for my wife and children. They're in a blue brake and they should have arrived at the Anchorage yesterday afternoon at the latest.' He gave them the registration number of Jeannie's brake.

'I'll check.' One of the soldiers went up to one of the parked lorries and spoke to someone inside. He returned with an officer. 'I understand you're looking for what was very likely the small party we escorted across the road yesterday,' said the officer, referring briefly to a small notebook. 'A young woman, three children and a dog, is that right?' David nodded. 'Making for the Anchorage, weren't they?'

Again David nodded, hardly recognizing a trickle of relief seeping through him. 'We couldn't allow them to go through with the brake,' there was a touch of apology in the officer's brisk tone. 'We've got the brake back there in the field.'

'They're on foot, then?' Clyde put in sharply.

''Fraid so. Frightfully sorry but orders are orders. Even women and children have to conform.' His tone was growing less official. 'We advised them to keep to the woods and keep a sharp look-out for any odd characters that might be roaming around. One of my own men went part of the way with them to make sure they got on the right path.'

David felt his heart thumping with fresh panic. 'You say this was yesterday?' he taxed the officer. 'What time of day was it?'

'Twelve hundred hours almost to the pip, I'd say,' replied the officer. 'Oh, by the way, one of my men came across this when he was doing a recce in the woods this morning. I guess it belongs to one of yours. It's a bit damp, I'm afraid,' he said ruefully, holding out the sodden Gruntly Finny.

It was a full moment before David could reach out and take the bear. Unaware of the circumstances, he wondered how it had come to be there. Could Heather or Susan have just helped themselves to Jeannie's bear? Clearing his throat he asked, 'Which way did they go from here?'

The soldier who had escorted Ruth pointed out the track and David and Clyde strode off immediately. Watching them, he turned to the officer, a worried frown creasing his brow. 'I'd have thought that party would have got to the Anchorage by now,' he observed. 'I hope to God they haven't run into any more trouble.'

David and Clyde searched the woods, quartering them and calling with all the strength of their lungs. They came to the big house but from the front entrance. They rang the doorbell repeatedly and when there was no response they peered in the windows. Seeing no sign of recent occupation they turned their attention to the outbuildings and, judging them to have been abandoned, they resumed their searching and calling and in a relatively short time afterwards, during a pause while they listened for the faintest echo of voices, they heard Ruth's sharp command to Tansy. Hurtling towards the sound they met the dog's excited rush to greet them almost at the same time as they saw Ruth and the children standing together as if frozen in flight.

'Daddy!' Forgetting their breathlessness the children ran to throw themselves into their father's arms but Ruth, shattered by mind-exploding relief and with her breath dragging against her chest, could only stand, her arms hanging limply at her sides, waiting for her husband to come to her.

After the first ecstasies of welcome had moderated, Clyde wandered a little distance from the group, pulling up short when he came across the man lying on the ground. His mouth twitched grimly as he saw the blood on the man's face and head and a few feet away the bloodstained bag of corned beef tins. Anger rose within him as he deduced what could have happened and lighting a cigarette he waited until it was half smoked before he rejoined the others.

'Something seems to have happened back there.' He tried to make his voice sound casual.

The two men listening to the children's awed account supplemented by shuddering interjections from Ruth felt their bodies stiffening with a vast rage. Their pulses raced with the primitive desire to kill, and striding to the place where the man lay they stood glaring down at the prone figure, their fists clenching and unclenching, their jaws set hard and mercilessly. Clyde, determined to quell his rage, knelt down and felt for the man's pulse, hearing the man moan as he did so. 'He'll be okay,' he pronounced. Rising to his feet he saw David's murderous expression. Quickly he reminded him, 'Better so, old buddie.'

For an instant David's glance was one of hostility and seeking to calm him Clyde lit another cigarette and offered it to him. But David turned away, struggling for control while the savage disappointment that the man was still alive became tempered with the knowledge that he would have wanted no one he knew to have been responsible for the killing. As Clyde said, it was better this way. He knew he must accept that. As he returned to where his wife and children waited in a huddle of questioning doubt, his rage continued to simmer inside him.

Clyde waited to pick up the bag of corned beef tins and tipping the tins onto the grass he held his lighter to the bag and let it burn, treading the resulting ash into the ground. Finding each of the corned beef tins was complete with key he opened them and roughly breaking up their contents scattered them for the birds and beasts of the woods to dispose of. The tins he then flattened with his foot before tying them in a handkerchief ready for dumping in the sea from the deck of *Moonwind*. Only when he was satisfied there was nothing more he could usefully do did he rejoin the rest of the party for the last stage of their trek to the farm.

David's mother was hovering at the farm gate with the attitude of one torn between the desire to rush to greet them and the need to keep an eye on her cooking. The children rushed forward, throwing themselves into her welcoming arms, but Ruth's footsteps dragged more heavily. She knew David had said nothing to his parents of Jeannie's death but she also knew they had to be told quite soon. How soon? As the question posed itself her mind rebelled. Dear God! Not now. Not at this moment of meeting! Was she herself not already too steeped in sorrow to have to witness the infliction of such hurt on another woman? On Jeannie's mother? Not now! Please, please not now! she wanted to cry aloud. Looking agitatedly up at her husband she met his grave eyes looking consolingly into hers, sharing her anguish. 'Not now,' he whispered as if she had indeed spoken aloud. She felt her head swim and her limbs become leaden. As David slid a supportive arm around her shoulders her tear-burdened eyelids released the flow of pent-up grief.

'She's had a rough time,' David explained to his mother.

'Indeed, I'm sure she has had,' she condoled. 'I was only thinking to myself how thankful I am that Jeannie's where she is and likely to be out of harm's way up there in the hills. At least these troubles shouldn't affect her there.' David's arm tightened around Ruth and the sudden rigidity of his body communicated itself to hers.

After the children had eaten and been coaxed upstairs to rest, David announced that he and Clyde were going down to *Moonwind*. Ruth jumped up fully expecting him to suggest she joined them but almost imperceptibly he shook his head. Instantly she divined the reason. He was going down to *Moonwind* where he would break the news of Jeannie's death first to his father and leave the old man to decide how and when his wife should be told.

'You should go and lie down yourself,' her mother-in-law advised when David had gone, and glad to escape the torture of possibly harrowing questions Ruth acquiesced meekly. Too keyed up to relax she lay on the bed only half listening to the sounds from the farm-yard and from the kitchen below. She would have welcomed sleep but she sensed that she was waiting for something and when her ears picked up her father-in-law's easily recognizable footsteps crossing the yard she knew what that something was.

In the kitchen the low murmur of voices was soon pierced by a sharp protest, so full of pain it made Ruth wince. Then all she could hear was the broken moaning of extreme grief. Ruth, trying to stifle her own great gulping sobs with the pillow, shut out all other sound from her ears until at last, shaken and exhausted, she was overtaken by sleep.

When she woke the house was abnormally quiet and she lay for some minutes half bemused and trying to convince herself she was waking from some ghastly dream. But reality pressed itself unrelentingly into her consciousness and she longed for the anodyne of more sleep. Rising she sponged her face with cold water and careful not to disturb the children she crept downstairs. At the foot of the stairs she paused to listen, fearful that her entry might be mistimed; that she might be about to intrude on grief of such intensity that it needed total seclusion. Hearing no sound she quietly opened the door into the kitchen, ensuring there was no one there before she entered. Through the wide open door into the yard a rectangle of late sunlight was spreading a mat of gold on the floor and as she moved towards it the sunlight was blotted out by the figure of her mother-in-law. For some seconds the two women stood dumbly as if suddenly transfixed, their eyes, full of wretchedness, holding each other's until, with arms outstretched they stumbled to embrace one another, clinging together as they tried to ease their mutual sorrow. The mat of sunlight narrowed and slanted away. The kitchen grew dim. Gently disengaging herself from Ruth's arms her mother-in-law stood up. 'There's still work to be done,' she said in a voice that was wrung dry of emotion.

15

At noon the following day a restored radio service was confidently proclaiming the resignation of the mainland government and the formation of a caretaker government which it boasted had already conceded all the demands of the rebels. The unions were unanimous in declaring the general strike to be at an end and in urging all workers to return immediately to their jobs. The proclamation, repeated half hourly with varying degrees of triumph, was extended during the course of the day to include reports of the speedy resumption of normal services, as well as to slip in sharp orders backed by sinister-sounding warnings to the nihilistic hordes who, it was clear, were refusing to abandon their campaign of destruction and looting.

The relief the news brought was, however, more than balanced by consternation when, later in the evening, television was back on their screens to present what was heralded as a 'forthright declaration of the policies of our new leaders'. The fears of those watching in the kitchen of the farmhouse were confirmed when there appeared on the screen the gloating faces of the politicians they most abhorred flanked by the union henchmen they most distrusted. With deepening disquiet they listened to the treacle-sponge voice of the so-called leader declaring the first edicts of the new 'People's Government'. They were shown shots of jubilant crowds gathering in city centres to celebrate the news of their victory. And they showed shots of former government ministers, who they claimed had already fled the country. Then the screen went blank again.

'The island to lose its independence and brought

into line with the mainland,' David's mother repeated. 'That's what he's threatening, isn't it?'

'He's been threatening that for a long time but I doubt he'll do it,' replied her husband.

'You reckon?' David's tone was dubious.

'I reckon,' his father said. 'The trades union bosses might pretend to go along with him but there's too many of them with money stashed away here and houses for bolt-holes ready for when the crunch comes,' his father retorted cynically. 'That's true,' he affirmed when David still looked doubtful. 'You ask any estate agent here.'

'I suppose he'll include the fishing industry in his talk of state ownership,' Clyde submitted. 'How d'you feel about working *Moonwind* under a boss, David?'

David swore under his breath. 'I'll be no government slave and I'll scuttle *Moonwind* before I'd let her get into the hands of that lot.' He thumped the table with such vehemence that Tansy leapt up from the rug on which she was lying and looked for an intruder to attack.

'There's always my country,' Clyde said, turning to include Ruth in his quizzical glance. The three of them had more than once discussed a proposal by Clyde that he and David should form a joint fishing venture based near his home in the USA, and because David had come to recognize that the fishing industry in the island was rapidly declining he had been tempted to reflect on such a possibility. It was always Ruth who had vetoed the suggestion, saying that they had their home and so many ties on the island they should at least wait until it became obvious that the decline was irreversible before they need think seriously of uprooting themselves. Now, Clyde's laconic remark affected her as if a door in her mind had begun to swing slowly open transforming gloom into light. Why not seize the opportunity and do as Clyde suggested? They had lost their home; Jeannie was dead; the immediate future threatened to be too bleak and possibly too dangerous to be endured; so why should they stay? Even if the venture should not prove a success the change of scene would give them time to come to terms with their loss; the preparations for departure allied to the sense of adventure would help prevent her mind from returning again and again to the experiences of the last few days. It seemed to Ruth that her thoughts had been spun on a roulette wheel which had now come to a decisive stop. Looking up, she met David's questioning expression. 'I think it's a good idea,' she said.

'We shall probably have to get going very quickly,' he warned. 'Once they start commandeering boats there might be no chance.'

Ruth caught her breath. 'You mean we should be going on *Moonwind*?'

'That's the idea,' David said. 'Why not?'

She looked at him steadily. 'I can be ready as soon as you are,' she told him.

After Ruth and her mother-in-law had gone to bed the three men stayed conferring and planning late into the night. The next morning, leaving the children in the care of their Granny, David and Ruth went aboard *Moonwind* where they talked a long time together, David pointing out the possible difficulties of the trip. The boat was roomy enough and with three capable adults, watchkeeping would not be too demanding. She gave him a reassuring smile. The daughter of a boatbuilder, she had had plenty of experience of the sea and now was undeterred by the problems which might confront them. When they returned to the farmhouse their faces were set with such resolve that David's father, meeting them as he emerged from the tractor shed, was in no doubt as to their joint decision.

'How soon?' was all he asked, bracing shoulders that

prior to being acquainted with Jeannie's death had shown no tendency to stoop.

'The day after tomorrow at first light,' David replied.

The old man showed no surprise. 'It's what I'd be doing myself if I were in your place,' he endorsed. 'You'll have the best time of year weatherwise.' He glanced towards the end of the yard. 'Lucky we got the diesel tank filled when we did. There'll be plenty of spare drums lying around the place too. I'll get a couple of the men to bring them up. And there's that sail old Herbie's been storing up in our loft for a while. We'll have to ask him first but he won't refuse, seeing he no longer has a boat.' He seemed to find relief in searching his mind for ways to help them.

As Clyde sauntered up to join them, Ruth went in search of her mother-in-law and found her sitting on her favourite seat in the orchard overlooking the small paddock where the children, with sporadic help from Tansy, were happily chasing butterflies. The old lady was sitting quite still and erect looking out across the sun-sequined water and all around her the last remnants of fruit blossom were drifting from the trees, studding the close-mown turf with flake-like petals. Ruth paused, letting the scene superimpose itself over the hideous memories of the past few days. How brave she is, she thought. How close I feel to her now, at this time of parting. As she stood wrestling with an oppressive feeling of guilt that they were about to desert her when she most needed them, her mother-in-law, sensing her presence, turned and beckoned her to the seat beside her. There was already too deep a sadness in the old woman's eyes for any deeper emotion to be discernible but as Ruth put an arm around her and told her of their plans she felt the tremor that ran through her taut body.

'We hate leaving you,' Ruth went on, her tone imploring forgiveness. 'Particularly just now. . . .' She

178

halted, thinking of Jeannie's funeral and the torture her mother-in-law must yet face. 'But Dave thinks we must go. He thinks they might freeze all assets and put an embargo on any boat leaving port without authority. Both he and his father think we must move quickly.'

The old woman reached for Ruth's hand and held it in hers. 'I wouldn't be wanting to keep you back,' she rejoined. 'I've lost a beloved daughter and, God knows, I don't want to lose an equally beloved son even though I know he wouldn't be lost to me forever like Jeannie. But he's right to go. His father says so. There's going to be no place in this country for a man who speaks his mind as David does.' She squeezed Ruth's hand. 'I can trust you to look after him for me.'

'I suppose you wouldn't consider coming with us?' Ruth knew the answer even before she had finished the question. Her mother-in-law stared straight ahead. 'Maybe we'll come and join you when we've tidied up things here,' she said evasively.

'We might not like it there and come home again quite soon,' Ruth responded. Come home where? her thoughts challenged, as a knifethrust of nostalgia reminded her The Braes was no more.

'That certainly could happen,' said the old woman. 'There'll always be a home for you here.' She stood up. 'You'll be needing stores and bedding for the journey,' she said. 'I'll go down right away and have a talk with Frank, the grocer.'

'The children are going to need more clothes than they have with them,' Ruth called.

'You won't get much in that line in the Anchorage,' her mother-in-law retorted. 'We'll just have to ask around the neighbours.'

Next day when the children were called in for their tea, David said, 'Now, sweethearts, I want you to listen very carefully to what I'm going to tell you.' The children regarded him soberly. 'Mummy and I want you

179

to have your baths now instead of going out to play. You must all go to bed very early tonight. Especially early,' he stressed. Silencing their protests he went on, 'This is because you have to be up very early in the morning.' The children glowered at him with puzzled resentment.

'How early?' they demanded.

'Before it's properly light.'

'Why?' The beginnings of apprehension clouded their eyes.

'Because we're all going to set out on an adventure. Mummy and I have been keeping it as a surprise but tomorrow morning we're going to go aboard *Moonwind* and set sail for America with Uncle Clyde.'

'America?' they squeaked, almost choking with excitement. 'All of us going to America for a holiday? All the way in *Moonwind*?' Their voices were ecstatic.

'Shall we be staying with Uncle Clyde?' Simon asked more calmly. His Uncle's stories of life in America had kindled in Simon a keen desire to see that country for himself. The vision of sailing there on his Daddy's boat was so rapturous it had entered his head only during his wildest imaginings.

David and Ruth exchanged glances of complete accord. There seemed no point in adding to the children's excitement and confusion by telling them at this stage they were not simply going for a holiday.

'Yes, we're going to stay with Uncle Clyde,' David agreed.

'How long will it take us?' Heather wanted to know.

'That depends on the weather and if we want to call in at any other ports on the way,' her Daddy told her.

'I hope we don't call anywhere,' cried Simon. 'I just want to go straight to America.'

Moonwind was provisioned and ready to sail. That night, after the last of the well-wishing friends and neighbours had left, Clyde, who with David intended spending the night aboard the boat, took his last farewell of David's parents. Taking the old woman's hand in his he looked hard into her eyes. 'I want you to know,' he began, blurting out his words as if for some time he had been battling with the compulsion to speak out, 'I'd come to hope I would be taking Jeannie back with me when I went home.' His voice grew rough. 'We . . .' Unable to trust himself further he bent and impulsively kissed her hand. Jeannie's mother reached up and putting both hands on his shoulders kissed him warmly on each cheek. 'We would have welcomed you as our son-in-law,' she told him. The old man gripped Clyde's hand, their gruff-voiced goodbyes revealing the extent of their emotion. A moment later the door closed as Clyde followed David out into the night.

Ruth awoke to a grey early morning light that was thickened by a cool, hovering mist which muffled the land in a silence pervaded only by the eerie booming of the distant foghorn. Opening the door to let Tansy out for her morning exercise Ruth felt the tiny droplets of mist like an astringent on her tired face. The day added to her sensation that she was continuing to move in a dream and she resorted to brushing her hair vigorously hoping the friction on her scalp would help to clear her brain. Rousing the children she supervised the last-minute preparations for departure so they were all sitting with quiet expectancy when David came to collect them.

'Everyone ready?' he asked.

'All ready,' stated Ruth firmly.

'Even Tansy's ready,' interposed Heather. 'I don't think she really wants to come to America because she keeps sneaking back to her chair. Granny's had to find me a lead to put on her.'

'Gruntly Finny wants to go,' declared Susan, cuddling the bear with which she had been reunited.

David's parents accompanied them to the pier and

there the last sad and yet glad hugs of farewell were exchanged before Ruth and the children and the slightly reluctant Tansy went aboard *Moonwind*. David disappeared below and almost immediately *Moonwind*'s engine throbbed into life. The cooling water from her exhaust sprayed into the sea. Coming up on deck David went into the wheelhouse and as soon as the engine revved Clyde untied the ropes from the bollards and leapt smartly aboard.

The final farewells were called. The exuberant waving of the children and the more restrained gestures of the adults continued as *Moonwind* nosed away from the pier, turned and made a broad sweep across the bay to head seaward.

On the pier the old people stood holding hands, maintaining their watch long after they could distinguish the shapes on board *Moonwind*, as, like a ghost ship, she merged into and then was finally absorbed by the distant gradations of grey that were composed of sea and mist and sky.

Bestselling Fiction

☐ No Enemy But Time	Evelyn Anthony	£2.95
☐ The Lilac Bus	Maeve Binchy	£2.99
☐ Prime Time	Joan Collins	£3.50
☐ A World Apart	Marie Joseph	£3.50
☐ Erin's Child	Sheelagh Kelly	£3.99
☐ Colours Aloft	Alexander Kent	£2.99
☐ Gondar	Nicholas Luard	£4.50
☐ The Ladies of Missalonghi	Colleen McCullough	£2.50
☐ Lily Golightly	Pamela Oldfield	£3.50
☐ Talking to Strange Men	Ruth Rendell	£2.99
☐ The Veiled One	Ruth Rendell	£3.50
☐ Sarum	Edward Rutherfurd	£4.99
☐ The Heart of the Country	Fay Weldon	£2.50

Prices and other details are liable to change

ARROW BOOKS, BOOKSERVICE BY POST, PO BOX 29, DOUGLAS, ISLE OF MAN, BRITISH ISLES

NAME...

ADDRESS..

....

....

Please enclose a cheque or postal order made out to Arrow Books Ltd. for the amount due and allow the following for postage and packing.

U.K. CUSTOMERS: Please allow 22p per book to a maximum of £3.00.

B.F.P.O. & EIRE: Please allow 22p per book to a maximum of £3.00.

OVERSEAS CUSTOMERS: Please allow 22p per book.

Whilst every effort is made to keep prices low it is sometimes necessary to increase cover prices at short notice. Arrow Books reserve the right to show new retail prices on covers which may differ from those previously advertised in the text or elsewhere.

Bestselling General Fiction

☐	No Enemy But Time	Evelyn Anthony	£2.95
☐	Skydancer	Geoffrey Archer	£3.50
☐	The Sisters	Pat Booth	£3.50
☐	Captives of Time	Malcolm Bosse	£2.99
☐	Saudi	Laurie Devine	£2.95
☐	Duncton Wood	William Horwood	£4.50
☐	Aztec	Gary Jennings	£3.95
☐	A World Apart	Marie Joseph	£3.50
☐	The Ladies of Missalonghi	Colleen McCullough	£2.50
☐	Lily Golightly	Pamela Oldfield	£3.50
☐	Sarum	Edward Rutherfurd	£4.99
☐	Communion	Whitley Strieber	£3.99

Prices and other details are liable to change

ARROW BOOKS, BOOKSERVICE BY POST, PO BOX 29, DOUGLAS, ISLE OF MAN, BRITISH ISLES

NAME..

ADDRESS...

....

....

Please enclose a cheque or postal order made out to Arrow Books Ltd. for the amount due and allow the following for postage and packing.

U.K. CUSTOMERS: Please allow 22p per book to a maximum of £3.00.

B.F.P.O. & EIRE: Please allow 22p per book to a maximum of £3.00.

OVERSEAS CUSTOMERS: Please allow 22p per book.

Whilst every effort is made to keep prices low it is sometimes necessary to increase cover prices at short notice. Arrow Books reserve the right to show new retail prices on covers which may differ from those previously advertised in the text or elsewhere.

A Selection of Arrow Books

☐ No Enemy But Time	Evelyn Anthony	£2.95
☐ The Lilac Bus	Maeve Binchy	£2.99
☐ Rates of Exchange	Malcolm Bradbury	£3.50
☐ Prime Time	Joan Collins	£3.50
☐ Rosemary Conley's Complete Hip and Thigh Diet	Rosemary Conley	£2.99
☐ Staying Off the Beaten Track	Elizabeth Gundrey	£6.99
☐ Duncton Wood	William Horwood	£4.50
☐ Duncton Quest	William Horwood	£4.50
☐ A World Apart	Marie Joseph	£3.50
☐ Erin's Child	Sheelagh Kelly	£3.99
☐ Colours Aloft	Alexander Kent	£2.99
☐ Gondar	Nicholas Luard	£4.50
☐ The Ladies of Missalonghi	Colleen McCullough	£2.50
☐ The Veiled One	Ruth Rendell	£3.50
☐ Sarum	Edward Rutherfurd	£4.99
☐ Communion	Whitley Strieber	£3.99

Prices and other details are liable to change

ARROW BOOKS, BOOKSERVICE BY POST, PO BOX 29, DOUGLAS, ISLE OF MAN, BRITISH ISLES

NAME..

ADDRESS...

....

....

Please enclose a cheque or postal order made out to Arrow Books Ltd. for the amount due and allow the following for postage and packing.

U.K. CUSTOMERS: Please allow 22p per book to a maximum of £3.00.

B.F.P.O. & EIRE: Please allow 22p per book to a maximum of £3.00.

OVERSEAS CUSTOMERS: Please allow 22p per book.

Whilst every effort is made to keep prices low it is sometimes necessary to increase cover prices at short notice. Arrow Books reserve the right to show new retail prices on covers which may differ from those previously advertised in the text or elsewhere.

Bestselling Romantic Fiction

☐ The Lilac Bus	Maeve Binchy	£2.99
☐ The Sisters	Pat Booth	£3.50
☐ The Princess	Jude Deveraux	£3.50
☐ A World Apart	Marie Joseph	£3.50
☐ Erin's Child	Sheelagh Kelly	£3.99
☐ Satisfaction	Rae Lawrence	£3.50
☐ The Ladies of Missalonghi	Colleen McCullough	£2.50
☐ Lily Golightly	Pamela Oldfield	£3.50
☐ Women & War	Janet Tanner	£3.50

Prices and other details are liable to change

ARROW BOOKS, BOOKSERVICE BY POST, PO BOX 29, DOUGLAS, ISLE
OF MAN, BRITISH ISLES

NAME..

ADDRESS ....

....

....

Please enclose a cheque or postal order made out to Arrow Books Ltd. for the amount
due and allow the following for postage and packing.

U.K. CUSTOMERS: Please allow 22p per book to a maximum of £3.00.

B.F.P.O. & EIRE: Please allow 22p per book to a maximum of £3.00.

OVERSEAS CUSTOMERS: Please allow 22p per book.

Whilst every effort is made to keep prices low it is sometimes necessary to increase cover
prices at short notice. Arrow Books reserve the right to show new retail prices on covers
which may differ from those previously advertised in the text or elsewhere.